TO BUST AN OPEN FLAME

Dan Zahn

To anyone who never read a book their damned English teacher assigned, this one is for you.

ACKNOWLEDGMENTS

This book would not have been possible without the support of friends and family, most notably Jan Marker and Eric Crisp, who encouraged me to follow my dreams, rather than play it safe. Thank you.

My first hit got him right in the gut. I watched his confused expression transform into pure fear. That should have made me cool it, but it was too late for that. My thirsty knuckles exploded his nose. Color sprayed across the cold spring air as he fell to the ground. His blood slowly swallowed my fist. I climbed on top and hit his nose again, this time from the other direction. I went on knocking it from one side of his face to the other, back and forth like it was silly putty. When my knuckles became raw I switched to kicking. I kicked so hard. Everywhere. I didn't hear the sirens. I couldn't hear anything. Feel anything. Not even when they cuffed me and took me away.

*****

The summer's sweltering sun forced sweat from every pore during the ride to LAX in the old rusty Ford Taurus. "Kris, I need your phone before you get on that plane."

I looked right into the jaded eyes of my probation officer, "You're joking, right?" I couldn't believe it. How in the hell was I supposed to last a month without my phone.

"You know the deal. You *do* know how lucky you are, don't you Kris?" Sarcasm. A typical companion to his cynical tone.

I told Mike, the overweight, tattooed, ex-gang member turned pencil pusher what he wanted to hear.

"I mean it Kris, if it wasn't for your teacher Ms. Sheridan, things would be a lot worse for you."

But what could be worse than getting shipped off to Alaska for the summer? I mean, yeah, of course being locked up in juvy was, but that was hard to remember as we entered the airport.

Mike kept on bugging me, "This is serious Kris, don't forget about your case plan. The things you have to do to complete the program. Here."

"What's this for?"

"This is the journal you need to complete. Don't be shy. The more you write the more it will help your case. Take advantage of any free time you might have, even if it is just a sentence here or there. It all adds up."

"I don't see how this is going to help you."

"Oh, you'd be surprised. But really, it is meant to help *you* Kris."

Like usual, he sounded like he was reading from a script. Saying what he was required to. The whole thing was a total joke.

"And remember, this is your last chance. If you get in a fight, or cause any trouble, the court system won't be so generous next time around."

Then he was quiet, lost in his own reflections. I watched him as we passed through security and found my gate. Like usual, he looked miserable. Beaten down from too many years of having to deal with guys like me. Eventually he regained focus and took a deep breath before he turned to me and said, "Try to enjoy yourself Kris." He said it with a softer tone than usual, which kind of threw me off for a second. "Really get to know the other kids in the program. They are all there because they want to be."

"Huh? You mean they didn't get in trouble like me?"

"No Kris, believe it or not, they even had to apply for this program. They want to be there. Their parents paid a lot of money for them to be there."

"So they are all a bunch of rich kids?"

"Some of them."

"Why?"

"Why what, Kris?"

"Why would anyone pay a bunch of money to go camping in the middle of nowhere?"

Mike laughed a little bit to himself. It was the first time in two months of dealing with him that I'd seen him even crack a smile. "Look Kris, none of these kids know who you are. You've got a great opportunity in front of you."

I stared out at the planes on the runway that were waiting for permission to disappear into the sky, "How so?"

"Well, this is a fresh start. You can reinvent who you are a little bit. No one knows your past, and they don't need to. Don't pretend. Just... just be a better version of yourself. The Kris you've always wanted to be."

A better version of myself. What the hell did that mean? Just then my flight started boarding. I couldn't wait to get away from this nut-job who all of a sudden was acting like all the other docs I'd been talking to lately.

He could tell he'd lost me and offered up one more piece of advice before I got on the plane, "Just try to get something out of this program Kris. You don't know how lucky you are."

I knew how lucky I was alright, how *lucky* I had been my whole damn life. I also knew this guy, this overweight, overpaid, and overopinionated employee of the state of California was full of crap. And I couldn't wait to be finished dealing with him.

"Kris, your cell phone."

Reluctantly, I handed it over. I felt like I was giving away a part of myself. "This should be illegal," I muttered under my breath.

Mike ignored my comment, "And remember, if everything goes well, your parents will be able to be here with me when you fly home. Your counselors will be waiting for you at the airport in Anchorage. Their names are Tyson and Andrea."

I walked down the boarding ramp, nervous for the unknown. I thought I heard Mike call out "Good luck" to me, but when I turned around he was long gone. Like usual, I was on my own.

DAY ONE:

3:30 pm: So here it is, my journal for this trip. Not sure what it is I am supposed to be writing about, but here goes nothing. For starters, I'm just sitting at the terminal cuz my ~~stupid~~ flight is delayed. First time on an airplane, and I gotta wait forever before we can even take off. This is so lame. Because of the delay, now I am gonna be the last one to arrive. Sucks.

Why I'm on my way to Alaska still doesn't make any sense to me. I guess somebody somewhere thinks that being out in nature will make me a better person or something. But the truth is, I couldn't give two craps about nature. I know what you are probably thinking right now, but trust me you are wrong. Yeah the court called this an opportunity, but let's face it, the only thing a court ever hands out is punishments. And this trip is no different.

And then there is this whole thing with the journal too, to keep track of my "feelings." What a crock. Talk about a total waste of time. As if that's not bad enough, I gotta meet up with some shrink and my probation officer after I get home and go back through the stupid journal so I can reflect on what I learned about myself from the whole experience. That's the last step before I can stop having to talk to all the quacks and my proby Mike, who seem to enjoy their sterile, stuffy rooms full of paperwork and machines that tell them what's wrong with everyone else but them. All I wanna do is move on with my life. Leave all this crap behind me.

By the time I was half way to Alaska I couldn't stop thinking about Mike's comment. I still didn't know what he meant by reinventing myself. The only thing I knew was that I was going to make sure that none of those rich pricks messed with me. The way I figured, we wouldn't have much of anything in common. So the less I got to know anyone else the better. Hell, I wouldn't even bother learning their names.

11:15 pm: Just landed. Crazy it's still light outside since it's almost midnite. Been sitting at the gate just waiting to unload. Crappy way to start a crappy trip I don't wanna be a part of anyways.

I saw one of my leaders as soon as I got off the plane. She held an old piece of torn cardboard with my name spelled wrong. I have a hard enough time showing respect to anyone in a position of authority already, but if these leaders can't even spell the name Kris right then they're not getting any respect from me.

Everything inside of me wanted to keep walking past her. Keep on walking and never be seen by anyone again. But she recognized my face. Must've seen a picture or something.

"Hi Kris, I'm Andrea, one of your Trip Leaders. Tyson is back at the campsite with the rest of the group. You must be exhausted."

"Nah, I'm fine." I tried not to make eye contact.

She stood there with a big old grin on her face for a while, like she wanted to hug me or something. It was weird and I kept my day bag in front of me as if to block her. Then the moment passed and she offered up, "Well then, shall we head to baggage claim?"

We got the rest of my stuff and drove off. I was tired and cold, and some pile of crap campground way up in Alaska was the last place in the world I wanted to be. Although I didn't really want to be back home either. Anywhere but here though, with eleven other kids I didn't even know. Didn't wanna get to know.

12:30 am: Got to the campsite and sure enough, all the other kids were already asleep. So now everyone knows everyone else, except me that is. Have to share a tent with two other boys. Can't fall asleep cuz one of them won't stop snoring. That's it for today. Not sure what else I am supposed to say.

DAY TWO:

8am: Woke up to the sound of rain. It is so cold and miserable. Luckily, the girl leader just came by and told us we get to sleep in and that the rain should clear out soon.

Since it never gets that dark in Alaska during the summertime, I guess it's not as important to get an early start as it would be in other places. So instead, we just hung out in the tent for a couple of hours. I wanted to try and sleep some more, but the other two boys wouldn't shut up. There's the fat one who snores, his name's Steve, and this other kid named Jeff. Jeff is from Chicago. He's really into acting, Jewish, and proud of it. The only thing he talks about more than acting and being Jewish is girls. You can tell he's too smart for his own good, which actually makes him kind of funny.

Then there's Steve. He's a chubby little bastard from San Diego who snores like an old lawnmower. He's done a million of these trips. He's crazy. Thinks he's some sort of photographer, too. Must've brought a couple grand worth of camera stuff with him. If it were up to Steve, he'd be hiking day and night, in the rain and snow. Hell, probably across water if he thought there was a chance he could make it. He's like a junkie for this outdoorsy crap.

While we were talking Steve asked, "So why did you choose this particular trip?"

I hesitated, not sure how much to say to them. Then all of a sudden I just blurted out, "I didn't choose jack, I had to go on this trip or they were gonna send me to jail."

That really got them going. The two of them asked a million questions and I tried to ration my answers wisely. I knew I was asking for trouble, but the clowns were hanging on my every word.

I got kind of carried away and told them I was a big fighter back home.

Steve's curiosity exploded, "But you're not very big. How are you so good at it?"

I could tell he was nervous after asking me, so I played off of it a little, "Want me to show you?"

He was almost shaking, and it took everything in me to hold back from busting out laughing. Instead, I played it real cool. I fed them some line about how strength had nothing to do with whether or not someone could fight. "It's what's inside that counts," I said as I tapped on my chest. Man did I have those two eating out of my hand.

10:30 am: Getting to know my tent mates, Steve (the one who snores) and Jeff a little better. I guess they aren't that bad, so far. The rain let off and now it's time to get up and meet the rest of the group.

Jeff and Steve told the other kids about how tough I was during breakfast, and most of them wanted to know all about it. I played it real cool though, and told them to get lost. That a fighter doesn't like to brag. I knew Steve and Jeff would do that for me from here on out anyways.

The group looked like a bunch of babies. They did. Like they belonged in some fancy neighborhood with rich parents who loved them. Parents who almost couldn't let their kids go to some far off place for the goddamn summer.

Their smiles and overall excitement made me sick. It was so phony. I knew they were all really just scared inside. I can tell these things. I'm pretty damn observant. And I'm smarter then I let on, just so you know. Sometimes it's just easier to fake it. And I'm telling you these guys were a bunch of phonies.

I told them my name was Holden. Holden Herb. They all believed me and half of them didn't even get it till the damn leader ruined it for me.

"Guys," she said, "This is Kris. He's from California."

Then she told us to wash our dishes. And that I had to help two other kids wash the group dishes from breakfast. I said that I had to go to the bathroom first.

I left the breakfast dishes unfinished and walked away. I needed to find a place to smoke. But as I was walking away the guy leader stopped me and asked where I was going. "I gotta take a piss," I kind of blew up at him, "Jesus, chill out. That *is* allowed here, isn't it?"

I kept walking past the bathroom till I came across a river full of disgusting looking brown water. It looked like chocolate milk. Really it did. I found a log with some privacy and smoked. By the time I got back to the campsite the tents were down and all the dishes were put away. All my stuff was lying on the ground where the tent I slept in used to be. Everyone else was in a circle with all their stuff.

11 am: I can tell the counselors already don't like me for no reason at all. I can't wait to get out of here. Had to learn how to pack a backpack because we are about to go on a five day hike in the backcountry. Five days with nothing but what we carry ourselves! Not looking forward to it. But first we still have to go over the rules.

What a joke. It was everything you would expect on a trip like this. No drinking or smoking, no hooking up, and on and on.

Basically, no fun.

The two leaders said we would get sent home if we got caught smoking, but I didn't give anything up, and don't plan to either.

2 pm: After lunch we all piled into a huge white van Steve has nicknamed "The Giant Marshmallow" and are driving up to some trailhead. One of the kids tried to watch me writing this stuff down, but I told him to mind his own business. ~~This is so stupid.~~

We finally made it to the trailhead and the funniest thing happened. It was so classic! As the twelve of us were unloading the van with the leaders, the ranger cop, or whatever they are called, told our leaders that there had been a brown bear sighting a couple days earlier at one of the places we were supposed to camp. Our guy leader said back to him, "Brown bears, eh? How about grizzlies? Seen any of them lately?"

The ranger pulled down his cheap Aviator sunglasses to reveal eyes of bewilderment. Then he said, "A brown bear *IS* a grizzly bear! I'm going to need to see your permits. Now."

We all got a kick out of how stupid our leader sounded. Nothing is better than watching someone in charge of you get in trouble by someone in charge of them. I did my best to make fun of him. Everyone was laughing, but the whole thing made me kind of nervous too. Who were these two leaders that were about to take me into the middle of no-where? It dawned on me that they might not know what the hell they were doing. Even worse, it seemed like I was the only one who noticed.

Then we put everything we didn't need in the van and started hiking. The clouds came in, but the rain held off. It felt like we were hiking in circles and I wondered when it would end.

9:45 pm: We just ate dinner and had a meeting that lasted over an hour! Talked about the day and each of our expectations for the trip. I didn't know what to say, so I didn't say much. The leaders tried to get me to talk more for a while but then moved on. Before sending us to our tents they made this big deal about putting anything with a scent in these plastic canisters we had to bring. Because of the bears. I think they are just trying to scare us. Well, I'm beat from hiking, but I don't know how I'm gonna fall asleep since it doesn't really get dark here.

Between Steve's snoring and the lack of darkness, it was impossible to fall asleep. At two in the morning I was still up. I couldn't stop thinking about how big of a deal everyone was making about bears. I've seen bears before at a trash dump my dad used to take me to in the mountains. I didn't see what the big deal was all about. Who cares what color bear it is. So I came up with an idea.

I got up and headed towards the pile of bear canisters. I opened one up and found some peanut butter. I spread it all over this rock. You know, so everyone would have a little show to wake up to. Feeling proud of myself, I went back to my tent and waited. Funny how much easier it was to fall asleep when I was really trying to stay awake.

DAY THREE:

7 am: Woke up to a bunch of the girls screaming. I guess a family of raccoons was trying to get into our food canisters. I wonder why?

I have to admit, when I first heard the screams I got real nervous something bad had happened. I realized maybe my idea wasn't so great after all. The two leaders scared off the raccoons and investigated the scene. I couldn't hear what they were saying, but I saw them pointing at the rock I rubbed the peanut butter all over. I thought for sure they were gonna try and find out who did it, but they didn't. They never even brought up the peanut butter. Instead, during breakfast, the girl leader casually mentioned, "That's why we bring those bear canisters, to protect our food from all the animals out here. I'm just glad that it was only raccoons this time. Though I doubt something like this will happen again."

She didn't say it in an accusing way, or anything like that. In fact, I doubt some of the other kids even picked up on it. But I knew exactly what she was saying. Message received.

9 am: After breakfast we started hiking. Then it started raining. Taking a quick break. I'm cold and soaking wet. This sucks.

The program that paid for my trip also bought me a bunch of fancy camping gear. Everyone else put on their rain jackets as soon as it started to sprinkle. Pansies. Then the girl leader called me out, "Kris, put your rain jacket on before you soak through."

"Nah, I'm fine," I said, "I can handle way worse than this."

"She's not asking," the guy leader stated firmly. "She's telling you. It's for your own safety."

"But I'm fine."

"Get it out and put it on," she demanded, and I could tell she was losing her patience.

Taking off my heavy backpack and putting it back on was gonna be a real pain in the ass. "But my jacket is at the bottom of my bag."

"We told you to keep it at the top of your backpack because we knew it might rain, remember?" He was much calmer than she was, and I hated that even more.

Of course I remembered. I just didn't do it because there wasn't a cloud in the sky when we were packing. In the end they made the whole group stop so I could take out my rain jacket. You could tell some of the other kids were getting frustrated with how much time the whole ordeal was taking. I hated the leaders for making such a scene. And I hated the kids who were getting frustrated. It wasn't my fault the leaders were being overprotective. And the best part was, as soon as I put on my jacket it stopped raining. I made sure to point that out to them, though they didn't seem to care much.

6 pm: Been hiking forever. Rain has come and gone all day. Feels like we are on a death march to nowhere.

All in all it was a pretty crappy day. I always figured that the whole point of being outdoors was so you could look at the mountains. But because of the rain clouds, I couldn't ever see more than a football field in front of me. So the whole time all I kept wondering was why we were even out here when it was so miserable and I couldn't see anything anyways. The guy leader overheard me bitching about it to one of the other boys while we were hiking. He just chuckled and asked, "So why do you think we are out here Kris?"

"Because you get some sick pleasure out of watching us suffer."

He just laughed. Then he said, "I don't want anyone to suffer, and I don't know why other people do this sort of thing. All I know is that I get a sense of accomplishment making it through a nasty storm like this. It reminds me of busting."

I didn't know what the hell he was talking about and it seemed like he was bating me into asking, but I didn't fall for it and kept walking. I just wanted to be done. I told him so and he laughed some more. That son-of-a-bitch was always laughing about stuff that wasn't funny. Then he said something about focusing on the journey, not the destination. He is a weird guy.

9 pm: Finally made camp. Ate cold soup for dinner. All I want to do is sleep but the counselors are making us have another meeting.

At our meeting after dinner, everyone talked about what a great day it was. I couldn't help but laugh at how dumb they all sounded. It reminded me how much I didn't want to get to know any of these people. I said as little as possible when it was my turn. I waited for the leaders to try and drag more information out of me, but they didn't. It seemed like they were already tired of me. That was fine by me. I was definitely tired of them. Tired of this whole damn thing.

DAY FOUR:

8 am: Woke up to the sound of rain. It is so cold and miserable.

After some warm oatmeal we started hiking again. The tents were still wet from the rain, and it felt like I was carrying an extra twenty pounds. After about a mile or so, we came across a river that we had to cross. It didn't look deep at all and was only about ten feet wide, but the leaders stopped us all and started making this big speech about safety and how to cross it the right way.

I didn't have any patience for what they had to say after they were wrong about me needing my rain jacket, so I just started crossing on my own. I figured this way I could cement my reputation as a bad ass with the rest of the group.

The first couple of steps were a piece of cake, so I looked back and hollered, "Come on guys, it's fine. They don't know what they're talking about, there's hardly a current at all."

That's when I fell over.

It was so embarrassing, and I didn't bother unbuckling the waist strap on my backpack like the leaders were telling us to, so now I was stuck on my back. I wasn't going downstream very fast, but I definitely couldn't get up because my backpack was like an anchor on the bottom of the river.

Next thing I knew, the girl leader was unclipping my backpack and helping me to the other side. I was soaked and the water was freezing cold. None of the other kids were laughing, but I could tell they were all holding it back. But that goddamn guy leader, he was doing that same chuckle to himself. I hated him for it.

My only saving grace was that four other kids fell crossing the river too, and you better believe that I laughed at every one of them when it happened.

The leaders decided to have an early lunch next to the river so our stuff could dry out a bit. I found some trees to hide behind and got totally naked. It sounds kind of funny to say this, but that was the first time in my life that I had ever been completely naked outside before.

12 pm: Still hiking. Don't know what else there is to say. About to climb a mountain.

After lunch, we got back to it. The clouds had all cleared out by now and there was a massive mountain looking down at us as we began to hike. One of the kids asked if we could climb it. The girl leader looked up at it, then at a map and said, "Yeah, the trail will take us up to the saddle over there," she pointed to a low point between the taller mountain and another one, "So we will take a break at the saddle and whoever wants to summit the peak can, so long as the weather holds off."

Getting up to the saddle was a real bitch. There were all these switchbacks winding up for a thousand feet. I thought it'd be quicker to just walk straight up, so I started cutting the switchbacks and making my own trail. Before I knew it I went from the last one on the trail to the first. Then the guy leader was all over me.

"Better stay on the trail Kris," he warned, "We don't need to start making any new trails out here. Besides, that will wear you out pretty quick going straight up with a heavy backpack on."

"I feel great, what are you talking about?" I said.

"It's also not very safe," and then he chuckled to himself as he added, "and the last thing you need is two accidents in one day."

His jab was subtle, but enough for a few of the kids to start laughing at. "What are you laughing at," I came back with, "You guys are going so slow we'll never make it to the top."

With that I started a light jog on the switchbacks. It didn't last long, but I was quite a ways in front of the rest of the group and it felt good to have some peace and quiet. When I made it to the saddle I was exhausted. I threw down my backpack and fell to the ground, basking in the sunshine.

It was a good ten minutes till the rest of the group made it to the saddle. When they got there, the boy who asked if he could climb to the top of the mountain didn't even look tired. "Can we still go?" he asked.

"Sure, whoever wants to can go. Leave your bags here though. We will stay here and watch them."

"Wait, you guys aren't going to come?" one of the boys asked the leaders.

"No, we trust you," the girl leader said, "Just don't do anything stupid and don't take longer than an hour. We still have five more miles to cover today."

"Five miles!" I said, "How far have we already gone today, six? Seven miles?"

That goddamn guy leader just chuckled to himself as usual and said, "Try two and a half. But the hard part is past us. It's mostly downhill or level from here on out...for the rest of today that is."

I sat back down and prepared for a nap till the boy who had been asking about the mountain said, "Aren't you coming with us Kris?"

I couldn't understand why anybody would want to do a bunch of extra work when we still had so much distance to cover. "Nah, you guys go on ahead, I'm gonna stay here and relax."

His response was simple, but effective enough, "I know it looks tough, but it should be pretty cool."

Hell yeah it looked tough. And I already sprinted up to the saddle to prove that I was tough. But I guess that wasn't enough. So I jumped up, sore as hell, and started for the summit. There were only four of us that went. Me, Steve, the boy who'd been asking, and some other kid.

The boy leading the charge was Matt. He was from Iowa I think. He was the golden child of the group. It was obvious that he was good at everything he tried, but he still managed to come off as humble. The worst part was that on top of everything else this kid had going for him, he was good looking too. You could tell all the girls were in love with him. I wanted to hate him strictly on principle, but he was so cool without being a dick about it that I couldn't help myself from wanting to be his friend too. Still, I played it cool anyways. I knew eventually I'd find something about Matt not to like.

Then there was Allen, the other kid who joined us. He was from upstate New York and a real nut-job. He was trying to pass himself off as a mix between a hipster and a hippy. He was also an environmentalist. At least he thought he was. What he really was, was a kid who was desperate to believe in something. Be a part of something. I've seen kids like him before, they're a dime a dozen back home. He was always going on about vegetarianism, veganism, and any other ism he had heard about.

Allen actually started to tear up a little when he saw the rest of us throwing our orange peels on the ground after lunch because we were "leaving a trace." He asked if any of us could see any orange trees around and then lectured us about the dangers of introducing foreign species to places like this. He went around picking up all of our peels, so I started tossing mine farther and farther away, leading him all over. It was pretty funny.

Allen's reason for being a vegetarian was because of the amount of water required to process beef. What a lame excuse! I mean, it's as if he doesn't even know what the hell he is talking about. Like he never thought about it, but instead was just reciting whatever crap he could remember from the latest documentary he watched. I mean, if you want to be a vegetarian or whatever, fine. But say it's for animal rights. Say it's for health reasons. Just say something that makes sense for chrissakes.

The best part was that even though Allen was vegetarian and a vegan, he was allergic to nuts. Now that I think about it, I actually feel kind of bad for him, because the one cool thing about the leaders was that they made everyone a bag of trail mix for the backpack. But not just any bag, this was the best trail mix I had ever seen.

You know how usually with trail mix, the only good part is one or two cashews and the M&M's, but before you know it there's just a bag of peanuts and raisins that nobody wants. Well with their trail mix, every handful was better than the last. Reece's pieces and peanut butter cups, chocolate covered pretzels, gummy bears, gummy worms, more cashews than any other nut, and all sorts of really good dried fruit. They must have spent a fortune on it. And poor Allen couldn't even try it.

Like Steve, Allen had been on a bunch of these types of trips before. The two of them wouldn't shut up about our leaders the whole way to the top of the mountain, and how much they liked them. Steve was going on and on about all the stories he had heard about our guy leader Tyson from his other trip leaders over the years. How crazy he was supposed to be, but in a good way. And how smart the girl leader Andrea was. I mostly kept my mouth shut, because they both seemed like tools to me. Like I said, their only saving grace was that trail mix they made. That and the girl leader had a pretty nice rack.

By the time we made it to about a hundred feet from the peak, I had a pretty bad headache and felt like I was gonna pass out. Then I threw up a little bit. Steve started thinking he was a doctor and asked me a thousand questions. I told him to shut up and that I was fine, but him and Allen insisted that I was dehydrated and might be dealing with altitude sickness.

"We should give him our water, rest a minute, then turn back." That was it. That was Steve's brilliant plan. I couldn't help but laugh in his face.

"Are you kidding, look how close we are," I argued, "That would be so gay to quit now. I'm fine, I swear."

There was no way we were going to get this close to the top and then quit just because of me. I knew I would never be able to live that down with the rest of the group. But then Matt said something I would have never expected.

"You guys," Matt started, "I don't feel so well either. I know we are close and all, but I want to head back, too."

I couldn't believe it. The golden boy wasn't so gold after all. I still wanted to finish, but now it was three against one, and it had already been forty-five minutes. So we all decided to take a minute to look around before heading back down. I couldn't believe that we had just decided to quit when we were so close to finishing, but I figured that maybe Steve and Allen knew what they were talking about if they were willing to turn around even though they felt fine. So I just sat there and looked around for a minute. I swear I could see for a hundred miles. Steve, of course, had his own map of the area and pointed out a bunch of crap including a lake off in the distance on the other side of the saddle. "That's where I think we are camping tonight, and that over there is where we started yesterday."

I could barely make out a dirt patch with some cars parked, and I have to admit that it was kind of cool to be able to see where we started from and where we were headed.

"This is the most beautiful thing I have ever seen," Allen shared, and I think he was tearing up a little bit. All three of them were in awe of the view.

"You guys look like a bunch of homo's right now, you know that?" I didn't really mean it like that, but the words just kind of flowed out of my mouth. Some sort of natural reaction for when I see guys showing their emotions, I guess. That's just how it is where I come from.

No one said anything back. Instead they just got up and started back down to the saddle. When we made it back to the rest of the group one of the girls asked Allen how it went. I was waiting for him to tell her how we couldn't make it because of me and Matt, but all he said was that it was a real beautiful view, and then changed the subject. In fact, no one said anything else about us not finishing, so I let it go too.

7 pm: Finally made it to our campsite. Never been so exhausted.

By the time we made it to the lake I was beat. Steve was still worried about me, so he set up our tent with Jeff on the condition that I would drink the rest of the water in my water bottle. I was supposed to be on the cook crew for dinner, but Steve said he would trade spots with me and then come get me when food was ready. It was pretty cool of him to do all that. I guess I could be friends with him after all.

DAY FIVE:

9 am: Slept great last night. Never even heard Steve snore.

I slept for thirteen hours straight. I couldn't believe it. Normally I don't sleep well. I have these nightmares that always wake me up. But I didn't even dream last night. At least I don't remember dreaming. I didn't eat dinner either. It was the first time that I felt good waking up in as long as I could remember. I was hungry as all hell though, and blueberry oatmeal never tasted so good.

11 am: The day was off to a good start till the "Leader-of-the-day" started bossing me around.

Each day the leaders pick one of us to be in charge of everything. Today they picked this jerk named Lyle. His dad is some big shot lawyer in Manhattan. All these kids are rich, but Lyle acted like he was the richest. He was a self-proclaimed gear-head, which basically means that he has all the latest and greatest equipment that you could possibly think of for the outdoors. But what's so funny, was that he didn't know how to use half the crap he's lugging around. I don't even think he knows what some of it is. But he acts like a know-it-all and refuses to let anyone teach him anything about his own stuff.

Like I said, today the leaders picked Lyle to be in charge and I wish they hadn't, because he gave me crap all morning. Assigning extra group gear for me to carry, telling me to go back and pick up trash from breakfast, all sorts of crap that doesn't have anything to do with me.

Lyle was one of those guys who just looks like a douche bag. He's got all the name brand clothes that are supposed to make you look cool, but he still didn't. Instead, he just looked like a poser. A real wannabe. And it didn't help that he was so tall and lanky. He's not very coordinated either, so he makes up for his physical awkwardness by acting smarter than he actually is. I'd love to knock him out and leave him for dead out here, but since I know that's not really an option I just told him to get bent when he tried telling me that I needed to stay with the group instead of walking up ahead of everyone else.

I stayed up ahead as far as I could get away with for the first half of the morning, until the trail disappeared. It really did. One minute it was there and the next it was gone. When the rest of the group caught up I suggested, "Well, since there's no more trail, I guess we can go back now, right?"

The girl leader looked frustrated as she explained to me, "This backpack route is a giant loop. We are not going back the same way we came."

I wished someone had told me that, because I hid some clothes back at our first campsite to lighten the load of my backpack. Nothing major, but I was still pissed no one told me.

"Remember," she went on, "when we showed everyone the topographical map of where we were headed and the places we would sleep at."

"No," then under my breath I said, "Like I care, this trip sucks anyways." She heard me but pretended like she didn't.

I do remember when she said that now, but it didn't seem all that important at the time. It's her fault anyways for not making a bigger deal out of it. Besides, when the leaders were showing everyone all that stuff I was using the outhouse at the trailhead because I knew there wouldn't be any bathrooms out here and the last thing I wanted to do was take a crap out in the woods.

Just thinking about that outhouse was reminding me of something that I had been trying to ignore for a couple of days now. You see, I hadn't gone, you know, since that day at the trailhead. We only had a couple more days out here and I was hoping to keep holding it till we made it back to the toilet, but now that I started thinking about it I couldn't stop, and I had to go pretty damn bad.

Here's the thing, when you have to poop out in the woods, it's a real pain in the ass. I mean it, literally. First you gotta find a spot where no one can see or might accidentally walk up on you, but you also don't wanna go too far away where you might stumble upon a grizzly or a moose. Once you find a good spot you have to dig a hole with this cheap little orange plastic shovel. Then, after you do your business, you have to cover it all up, but not with the shovel. With sticks. See, there's only one shovel for the entire group, and when you bring it back, to make sure you didn't let it get anywhere close to the poop, you have to hand it back to the Leader-of-the-day holding on to the part of the shovel that goes into the ground. But that's not even the worst part. The leaders said we weren't allowed to bring any T.P. because it leaves a trace that people were there. Personally, I think that my poop does a pretty good job of taking care of that already, but what do I know. So instead of using T.P. you gotta use leaves, sticks, twigs, smooth rocks, basically whatever you can find to get the job done.

For all of these reasons, and the fact that I would have to ask Lyle for permission to go crap in the woods, I was doing my best to hold it. But it was rapidly becoming apparent that the time had come. So I headed off into a section of forest to take care of business while the rest of the group caught up and figured out where we were supposed to go. All I can say is, after how nervous I had been about the whole ordeal, it really wasn't as bad as I thought it would be. Not that I liked it, but I know I could do it again if I had to.

When I came back to the group, Steve and Allen tried to give me a hero's welcome. They kept saying how proud they were for me, and reminiscing about their first time going poop in the woods. It was all real weird and I told them to shut up and leave me alone. But they were both so excited for me I eventually let them enjoy the moment. Those guys were never gonna get laid if they thought it was a good idea to talk about other people's poop in public. It grosses me out just thinking about it.

3 pm: Kept hiking. We all would have got lost, but I found the way.

The leaders told Lyle which direction to lead us in, and we started pushing deeper and deeper into a new section of forest. The trees were becoming tighter every step, and everyone's backpacks kept getting caught up in branches. Lyle was doing a terrible job picking a path, and I was happy to let him know. "You think you can do better Kris," he said to me, frustrated as all hell, "Be my guest. You lead the way for a while."

I told him I'd be happy to, and quickly found a game trail for us to follow. A game trail is just a small trail made by animals over time. The guy leader said that he was real impressed with how well I was navigating us through the trees, but that I had to slow down so that the group didn't get separated. Before long, he was right behind me making sure I didn't go too fast. After about a half hour or so we took a break so that everyone could catch up.

Whenever the guy leader would go up ahead to scout out the next section, he would ask me if I wanted to tag along instead of asking Lyle. I could tell this drove Lyle nuts, which was the only reason I kept agreeing to go. By late afternoon we had made it through the woods and arrived at our campsite. A couple of the kids told me I did a good job leading the way. Lyle got super jealous and kind of threw a fit. It was embarrassing for him. It would have been easy to make fun of him, you know, to really drive it in, but I figured he had done enough on his own so I let it go.

10 pm: I was beat by the time we started our nightly meeting but managed to stay awake. These long days really take their toll. I said that it felt good to help find the trail and that I had a good day when it was my turn to talk.

DAY SIX:

9 am: Had another good night of sleep. Must be cuz I'm so tired by the time I hit the sack. As for today, guess what we get to do? Hike all day! Big surprise, right? Same old ~~shi~~ crap, different day. Oh yeah, and tonight I am in charge of cooking dinner.

The good news was that we got to our campsite early with plenty of time to relax. Most of the group went off exploring. I hung out in my tent and tried to take a nap.

Since Steve had switched me spots for cook crew, now it was my turn to help prepare dinner. It was me, Jeff, and this other girl on the cook crew. The girl was pretty cute, but she acted like a bitch when I tried to flirt with her on the day we drove to the trailhead. So I pretty much ignored her until now. But it sure would be nice to hook up with a girl like her.

The funny thing was, now that I was ignoring her and she heard the other boys telling everyone that I was a fighter, she seemed more interested.

"I heard you are pretty tough back home, is that true Kris?"

I was trying my hardest to play it cool, but every part of me wanted to melt in her hands. "Sometimes."

It was all I could muster up, and I felt like an idiot for saying it. But it kept her interest and fortunately Jeff jumped in and started bragging a little for me. She started asking more questions, but then I interrupted her with, "Wait a second, what's your name again?"

I thought it was pretty smooth and she played right into it, getting all worked up. "Kris," she started, "How do you not know everyone's name by now? We all know yours."

I kept trying to play it cool and threw in, "Yeah, maybe that's 'cause I'm the type of person everyone seems to know and you're just someone who people forget about easily."

Right away her eyes puffed up and I could tell she was fighting back tears. I felt real bad as soon as I said it and quickly dropped the cool-guy act. I tried to make up for it by adding, "plus I'm real bad at remembering names, I think I got some sort of learning disability or something."

She looked at me, like *she* felt bad because I said that part about a learning disability (which was crap anyways), and answered, "Jennifer."

It was pretty quiet the rest of the time we were cooking. Except for Jeff of course. He went on and on about all the drama girls he'd hooked up with and all the places in the theatre that would be perfect for having sex. Normally I would have loved to hear all about it, but I felt real bad about hurting Jennifer's feelings. Hell, maybe all the people she cared about really had forgotten about her. Or maybe they wanted to, and that's why they sent her way the hell up to Alaska for the summer. Worst of all, I couldn't tell if it made her like me more or just plain hate me all-together, but I figured she probably hated me for good now. Which was fine by me the more I thought about it. Just one more person I didn't have to worry about.

After dinner we had our nightly meeting up on this hilltop where we could see forever in every direction we looked. I guess it didn't really matter which way I did look, because it was just a bunch of mountains, but it was kind of cool to me that we hadn't seen any signs of people for a few days now. No cities, no car horns honking, nothing. Just the sound of the wind, and an occasional screech from a bird flying high above us.

The meetings that we had every night were really lame. They reminded me of a group therapy session or something. We all sat in a circle and were each supposed to talk about a highlight from the day, and then name someone who was our hero for the day. And we had to say why too. So far I hadn't had a hero, but I said mine was Jennifer because she taught me how to make Mac'N Cheese. The truth of it was that I already knew how to make it, I mean I practically lived off of the stuff back home, but it made her smile and that made me feel kind of good I guess. Maybe there was a chance I could still hook up with her.

Then after everyone was done sharing their highlights and heroes, the Leader-of-the-day gets to pick a question that we all have to answer. Tonight, Matt was the leader and asked, "What's the hardest thing you have ever done?"

Everyone was giving pretty lame answers. Answers that they thought were real good, but didn't sound very impressive at all. Except this kid Paul. He is without a doubt one of the strangest kids I have ever met. He's from the east coast, I forget exactly where though. But he is possibly the clumsiest person in the entire world. His answer was short and simple. "The hardest thing I've ever done is go number two out here in the woods. I tried to lean up against a tree, but I ended up falling. Thanks again guys for not teasing me too much about it, and thanks Matt for letting me borrow your extra pair of pants."

"Um, don't worry about it Paul," Matt awkwardly responded, "You go ahead and keep them."

Paul looked like it was the best present anyone had ever given him. No one laughed at his story. Instead we were mostly just grossed out at the thought of him falling into his own crap. The other reason no one really laughed was because it just would have been too easy with a kid like Paul. So much so that no one ever gave him too hard of a time. Besides, he was usually in his own little world and wouldn't notice anyways. I wondered how Paul would have been treated back home.

When it was the guy leader's turn to answer he took a long time before he said anything. You could tell that Steve and Allen were waiting for some epic adventure to be revealed, one that would confirm all of the stories they had heard about him from their past trip leaders.

But instead all they got was a single word.

"Busting," he finally said in a soft voice full of reflection, like he was in his own world too.

Everyone started to giggle for obvious reasons. He didn't seem to mind, didn't even seem to notice. Finally one of the girls asked him what he was talking about. Jeff chimed in, "I'd be happy to show you," and all the boys started 'busting' up with laughter.

After it quieted down again, the leader began to explain, "Busting is when you start a fire without matches, a lighter, flint, or anything like that. Just friction."

"I always need some friction before I can bust too," Jeff whispered, but this time only a few of us laughed.

The leader continued, "Busting is something that I have tried many times in my life, but only been able to do once."

"When was that?" Matt asked.

"When it mattered most. You see, I was rock climbing with a few friends and this girl, her name was Emily, she broke her femur. We couldn't move her because the hike in to where we were climbing was very steep, so my other friend went for help."

"How come you didn't just call for help?" interrupted one of the girls.

"There was no cell phone service where we were, just like how there isn't any here either."

The sudden realization of not being able to call for help if we needed it while we were out here made me feel vulnerable and filled me with anxiety. I guess I just assumed the leaders had some sort of a satellite phone or something.

He continued, "Like I was saying, it was a very long and steep hike back to our car. We were only planning on being gone for the day and had packed extremely light. But it was late afternoon when she fell and it was clear that the two of us were going to have to spend the night out there till our other friend would be able to return with a ranger and the equipment needed to carry her out of there safely. I was able to stabilize the injury to help reduce the pain, but that night it got very cold. I knew that if I couldn't start a fire there was a very good chance that she could die from hypothermia. So I focused all of my energy, and eventually was able to bust an open flame."

And that was it. That was his whole story. I couldn't help but feel gypped. After a minute or so of silence Steve asked, "Did she live?"

"Yep."

"So you haven't been able to start a fire like that since?" asked Matt.

"I haven't tried."

"Why not?" asked Jennifer.

"I guess I haven't needed to. I know now that I could do it if I really needed to. And that is good enough for me."

Then Matt asked, "Will you show us how to do it?"

"Yeah, I can teach you guys the basics of it. Maybe on our river rafting trip. But I have to warn you that it is very difficult."

I could tell that everyone thought *they* were the exception to the rule. It made me sick watching them ignore the obvious fact that they would surely fail. As for me, I had no interest at all in any of it. The only thing I learned from the story was that I should always carry a lighter.

By the time it was my turn to answer the question I was pretty bored. "What's the hardest thing I ever had in my life? Hardest? Well there is one thing that's pretty hard." I stared at the girl leader's giant boobs and made sure she knew what I was talking about, "Yeah, it's especially hard sometimes in the mornings, but I usually manage to over-come it."

I couldn't help but start laughing. A couple of the other boys laughed too. The girls looked pissed, even though I think they thought it was funny too. But boy did the leaders hate it. The guy told the next person to answer. "Wait," I pleaded with him, "I can *handle* it, I swear," but even as the innuendo came out of my mouth I started busting up again, and this time so did everyone else, which really pissed off the leaders. They wanted order. Nice, honest answers that would inspire the rest of us. But now everyone else was laughing with me, they were on my side and it felt good.

The meeting slowly dragged on, but now the leaders had given up and were just trying to wrap things up. I had won. We had won.

8:30 pm: I hope we don't have to do nightly meetings every day. They are like torture to me. Can't wait to get into the tent.

After the meeting the guy leader pulled me aside and asked me why I was always trying to be such a smart ass. I gave him the typical, "I dunno."

Then he said, "The best meeting we have had so far was the one that you slept through a couple nights ago. If you don't want to be here, that's fine. I have no problem taking you to the airport as soon as we get back to the van tomorrow if that's what you want. Is it?"

I just stood there.

"Is that what you want?"

"No."

"No what?"

"No, sir?" I wasn't sure what he was looking for.

"What? No, that's not what I meant."

"Fine, what do you want me to say? Just tell me what you want me to say and I'll say it, Jesus."

"Kris, there isn't anything specific that I am looking for here. I want you to be honest. Not just with me. But with yourself. Do you know what I mean?"

"Yeah." But really I had no idea what he was talking about. Honest about what? All I knew was that I didn't want to talk anymore. He finally gave up and I went straight to the tent. Jeff was full of compliments, but Steve was a different story. He looked like he was disappointed. But I didn't care what he thought. Instead I relished my victory with Jeff till we fell asleep.

DAY SEVEN:

7:30 am: Woke up to the rain again. Why do people do this to themselves?

It was really coming down. But this time we had to take down our tents and pack everything up while the rain poured down on us. It was miserable. Then we got lost. It was crazy how a trail could just disappear, but they did all the time. We eventually found a game trail and stayed on it till we came across a moose.

9:45 am: Just saw a moose. The thing was massive! The leaders seemed pretty ~~nervis~~ nervous about it all. Kept going on and on about how a moose can be more dangerous than a grizzly.

After the moose got tired of staring at us and walked off in a different direction than we were headed I told Steve, "I can't figure out why people purposely put themselves in places like this where they have to worry about getting attacked by grizzlies and moose, and who knows what else."

The guy leader overheard and just gave his usual stupid chuckle, then added, "You think that you are much safer in a city? Personally, I'd rather take my chances out here."

That shut me up real quick. Suddenly I didn't feel like talking about it much anymore because I knew he might be right.

11 am: Still hiking. The rain finally began to let up and it seems like we can't possibly have much farther to go.

But what did I know. I was kind of zoned out, just marching on and on as if the trek would never end. I couldn't help but feel like one of those refugees I always hear about. You know, the ones in places like Africa who have to leave their homes and can only take what they can carry. I know it's totally different, but like I said, I was zoning out and it sure felt real to me. And then we came across a rotting corpse.

I had never seen anything like it. The rib cage was all exposed and the insides were eaten away. The leader said that it was the remains of a full grown moose and must have been dead for a couple days already. Call me crazy, but I was suddenly way more scared of a grizzly than a moose, no matter what the statistics said.

Jennifer started to freak out, so I told her it was fine, "I mean, whatever did this must be nice and full now, right?" I was telling myself as much as I was telling her.

Then, one of the girls pointed out to Paul that he was standing in a huge pile of crap. He looked down and said, "Oh shit!" and then mushed around in it a couple of times before actually stepping away from it.

Paul was something else.

Allen asked the obvious question that we all were afraid to know the answer to. "Do you think that pile of poop is from a grizzly bear?"

The guy leader transformed his chuckle into a loud rumble of laughter as he answered, "Well geez Allen, it looks like it belongs to a brown bear to me. Too bad a ranger isn't around to tell us all about it."

It was pretty obvious that what Paul had been standing in was bear crap, and you could tell everyone was nervous. But the guy leader's joke helped ease the situation a little. Then the girl leader tried to calm us down by adding, "It's all right everybody, this bear scat is old. There's nothing to worry about, I'm sure this bear is long gone now. If this looked fresher, then I might be concerned."

So we did the only thing we could do, we pushed on. The sun was finally out and I tried to focus on the warmth that it was providing. But the only thing on my and everyone else's mind was the thought of coming across a bear. I couldn't believe I actually tried to attract one with the peanut butter a few days back.

We had to hike through this section of tall grass and there were giant imprints from where an animal had recently been laying down. A grizzly? Who knew for sure, but I guarantee every one of us assumed so. The leaders told us to be as loud as we wanted so that if there was anything in front of us, it would hear us coming and we wouldn't startle it. It was that whole, 'the animal is more afraid of you than you are of it' thing, but no one seemed to be buying it because everyone was dead quiet. Then the worst thing that could have happened did.

We came across more bear poop, but this time it was fresh. So fresh it was still steaming. It would have been better to just have a bear jump out and get it over with than to deal with the anxiety we were all experiencing. Now even the leaders were having a hard time keeping their cool. You see, the problem was the game trail we were on just kind of stopped at this giant pile of bear poop. Without a trail, we could only see a foot or two in front of us through the tall grass, which highly increased our chances of stumbling across something we didn't want to. We still had to push through a good hundred feet of tall grass before we could get to a creek we needed to cross. We couldn't see it, but I knew we were close because I could hear the water rolling off of the rocks.

We all pushed on, one step at a time until we made it to the creek. It was the scariest hundred feet I ever walked in my life, let me tell you. When we got to the edge, it was clear that we couldn't cross from where we were at. Since I was always at the front of the pack, the guy leader turned to me and said, "I'm going to scout out the creek and look for a place to cross, you want to come with me?"

I don't know why, but the word "Okay" somehow managed to find its way from my mouth to his ears. As we started walking upstream, I was kicking myself for agreeing to go.

"I can't believe you said you wanted to come with me," the guy leader said, "I was kind of joking because I didn't think you would say yes."

What the hell! This guy's joke was about to get me killed. I wanted to yell at him but I tried to play it cool, "Yeah, well I'm not a little bitch like all those rich kids back there."

"You hate them because they are rich?" he asked.

He caught me off guard with that one. I didn't know what to say. I stumbled around with my words and then finally gave a, "I dunno, kind of."

"I understand," he said, which was an even bigger surprise. "I used to feel that way too when I was younger. I hated it whenever I heard someone say that money couldn't buy happiness. They had obviously never been broke before, right?"

It had never dawned on me that the leader didn't grow up like all these kids. "So you don't like them either... man? Then how come you do it? Work with them?"

He interrupted me before I could finish, "You still don't know my name, do you?"

I felt like a jerk the way he was calling me out.

He went on to spare me the embarrassment of admitting it, "It's Tyson. And the girl leader is Andrea. Do me a favor and try to remember, okay? That is, if we make it out of here alive."

His usual chuckle was more nervous and this time it was contagious. I told him I would remember. After a minute or two of silence he finally answered my question. "I do like these kids. If there is one thing I have learned, it is that everyone has issues that they are dealing with. I don't care how good someone's life looks on paper; everyone has legitimate struggles from time to time."

I didn't say anything back, so he added, "I can't imagine that you believe me right now at this point in your life, and that's okay.

But I hope one day you will understand. That's why I do this job, because believe it or not, you aren't the only one who needs to learn that lesson."

The way he said it I knew that he was being dead serious, and for the first time I began to think about Tyson a little differently. I've never really respected anyone in a position of authority before. Don't get me wrong, I still didn't respect him; he was kind of an idiot if you asked me, but I felt like I understood him a little better. And that's saying a lot because, come to think of it, I don't think I have ever tried to understand any of the authoritative figures I've had to deal with.

All of a sudden Tyson got real serious and said, "Look!"

Right in front of us was a perfect place to cross the stream. "Sweet," I said, "Want me to go get the group?"

"No. It's not that. Look. In the mud."

I looked down in the mud at the bank of the creek. Clear as anything there were giant paw prints with huge claw marks digging into the mud. I was convinced that at that very instant a giant grizzly bear was going to stand up out of the tall grass and swat Tyson's head clean off before turning its attention to me.

I couldn't believe I was probably about to die from a bear attack out in the middle of nowhere. I knew there was a reason to hate the outdoors: because it could kill you, that's why. This trip was going to be the death of me, I knew it.

Tyson pulled out this tiny little pocket knife and a can of bear mace. I told him that I doubted his ability to save us with the available weapons.

"Having doubt in yourself from time to time is okay. The trick is not to give up hope," then he looked at me and gave me his usual chuckle as he admitted, "I think the only thing this stuff will do is piss off a grizzly, but hey, I guess you have to work with what you are given sometimes. Know what I mean?"

There was something about the way he said it, like he wasn't talking about bears at all. Like he was talking about life. My life.

His hand with the knife was shaking. Not a lot, just barely enough for me to notice. He was still chuckling, as if he was laughing at himself and the situation he found himself in. I don't know why, but it made me feel better. I was scared too, but his acceptance of the situation he was in was somewhat comforting. Then he added, "Besides, these tracks are coming from the other side of the creek, this bear is probably long behind us by now."

And then, just like that, he smeared the claw marks into the mud. This was the only acceptable place to cross the creek, bear tracks or not. He knew it and so did I. But we were the only ones who would need to know about the tracks. Tyson called for the rest of the group to come over and then we crossed the creek one by one, till we were all safe in the open field on the other side.

We didn't run into a grizzly that day. And no one else had any clue about the fresh bear tracks in the mud. Hell, no one even seemed to notice that Tyson was carrying his pocket knife and a can of bear spray. He looked so silly, because he was right. All that crap would have done was pissed off a grizzly if we had come across one. But I guess he was right about something else too, sometimes you have to work with what you have.

Most of the rest of the hike was bushwhacking until, out of nowhere, a trail just kind of picked up again right in front of us. It was the weirdest thing because we were all convinced the leaders had gotten us lost. But they seemed to know where we were all along after all.

3:30 pm: Finally made it back to the trailhead and our van. Driving back towards Anchorage now so we can clean up and eat dinner.

I never thought I would be so happy to see signs of civilization. Music never sounded so good as it did blaring from our van's speakers while we drove towards Anchorage. But with everyone crammed in the van it quickly became apparent that we all stunk. I mean it, we really smelled bad. No one seemed to notice out in the backcountry, but now the stench was inescapable.

We drove to our next campground, showered, then set up camp. But instead of having to cook our own dinner, the leaders, I mean Tyson and Andrea, surprised us and took us into town for pizza. It was quite possibly the best meal of my life.

After that we found a dollar theatre. We watched one of the old James Bond movies. It was really cheesy, but I wished that someone like that had been on the trail with us today. What made Bond so great was that he had absolutely no fear, and he never doubted himself either. Doubt equaled weakness to a real hero.

DAY EIGHT:

6 am: We woke up extra early today and are headed south to go sea kayaking. The drive is 4 hours and we just went through a tunnel that must have been a mile long!

You'd think the long drives would be the worst part of the trip because everyone's crammed so close together inside our van. But I didn't mind them at all. Especially this one. I sat in the far back and Jennifer ended up falling asleep on my shoulder. I could see down her shirt a little, but it mostly just felt nice having her lean up against me. I couldn't stop smelling her freshly washed blonde hair. It smelled like privilege and opportunity. Or at least what I figured a life like that would smell like.

I tried to hide how into her I was, but she could tell anyways. She had an overfed ego because of all the attention boys gave her, and she thought that gave her the authority to act like a bitch all the time. Except when she wanted something, then she would get just flirty enough to fool you into thinking there was a chance. As soon as she got what she wanted, she went right back to bitch mode.

I found myself ignoring the fact that she was shallow and lacked any sort of real personality. Instead I fantasized about what the sex would be like. That's a lot of power for a girl like that to have over guys. Why couldn't she just be sweet like some of the other girls? And why couldn't *they* be as hot as her? Or would they just turn into bitches too? If only Jennifer knew how people really felt about her, maybe she would start caring about her personality as much as she did about her hair. I'd tell her myself, but I still thought there was a chance we might hook up. Am I a sucker? I am a sucker. God I'm a sucker.

On the other side of me was Jeff. He was full of his usual gross stories and funny jokes. We mostly just talked about drinking and smoking, and I think Jeff is the only other kid who smokes besides me on this trip, even though most of the kids like talking about it.

When we got to the end of the road there was this sea kayak guide who was waiting for us in an empty parking lot. "You're late," was all she said when we pulled up and you could tell that she was in a bad mood. Tyson tried joking around with her a bit but she wasn't having any of it. So he gave up and unloaded our stuff from the roof rack, that's where all our gear goes, while Andrea tried sweet talking her. Andrea seemed to have better luck.

After a long and boring safety talk we packed up our kayaks with enough gear for a few days and pushed off into the freezing water. It was mind-numbing. All we did was paddle, over and over, all day long. I don't think anyone was enjoying it to tell you the truth. Kids would start lagging behind and the guide lady would yell at them, then yell at Tyson and Andrea, then yell at the rest of us. It would really suck if our leaders yelled as much as the guide lady did.

4:30 pm: We ~~eventuly~~ eventually paddled our kayaks all the way to this island in the middle of nowhere. It has these huge trees. I've never seen anything like them before. And in between them are these wooden planks and platforms where our tents go.

I decided to call it Ewok Island because it reminded me of the Ewok village from the *Star Wars* movies. There were lots of places where I could have some privacy and I decided to ask Jeff if he wanted to sneak off and smoke with me. I couldn't believe he turned it down. Said he was scared of getting caught and being sent home. I told him he was a poon and went exploring on my own.

10 pm: Tonight we got to have a campfire for the first time on the trip. I love fires. Not just for the heat. They

are so simple, but I could stare at them forever. It's easier to think around a fire.

Tyson got yelled at for making it way too big. He looked like a natural-born-pyro and we were all egging him on to keep making the flames grasp higher into the sky, till we could no longer distinguish between the embers and the stars that were trying to outshine the bright midnight sky. But the guide lady was pissed. I asked Tyson, "What do we need her for anyways? Can't you and Andrea just take us around?"

He tried to defend her even though I could tell he didn't like her either. He said that it had to do with the permits for accessing the wilderness area we were in, and how we would be using specialized guides for lots of other parts of our trip.

"Like what?" I asked.

"You know, when we do our ice climbing and river rafting. Andrea and I know how to do all that stuff, but we use experts for safety and insurance reasons."

"You mean we are gonna go ice climbing?" I asked.

He gave his usual chuckle, although it didn't bother me as much anymore. He started explaining more about the trip, but soon I was distracted by the flames and started to tune him out. He could tell, and was ready to get back to his fire anyways. I think he likes fire more than anyone else I have ever met.

DAY NINE:

9 am: Today we woke up early and then paddled to the edge of a glacier field. As we got closer we passed giant icebergs that were floating in the water.

The way that the icebergs get there is they fall off from the cliffs of the glaciers. Allen thought he was an expert on the matter, and told us it's called calving. I didn't care much about that though. I was too busy ramming the icebergs with my kayak. You see, there might only be a small piece of ice sticking out of the water, but that could just be the tip of a giant chunk of ice the size of a car—or bigger—that is underneath the surface of the water. When you hit the part that is above the water, if the iceberg is the right size, you can make the whole thing flip on its side.

Of course the guide lady yelled at me as soon as she saw me doing it. She wouldn't shut up about how dangerous it was and how easily one of them could flip me over, and how cold the water was, and on and on. Go figure the one thing about nature that I think is actually cool I am supposed to stay away from.

She was really giving it to me and I thought she'd never stop. Then Tyson paddled over and she started giving it to him instead. About how he should have better control over his students. That didn't go over very well with him and he started getting all philosophical with her. "That iceberg represents the world to a guy like Kris."

I thought to myself, "It did?"

Tyson went on, "The tip above the water represents his perception of the world, but everything else below the waterline, that represents reality. Kris was only trying to knock the iceberg on its side to catch a glimpse of reality, unaware of how dangerous it can sometimes be. And now that he has experienced so much of your wrath I am confident he will take it easy when it comes to ramming icebergs."

That shut her up real quick.

The truth of it was that none of that stuff he was saying ever crossed my mind, but I couldn't stop thinking about it for the rest of the day. I wasn't sure I knew what he was talking about.

When we arrived at our campsite on the edge of the glacier field I told Steve about it and asked him what he thought Tyson meant. Steve thought about it for a while, and then said that he figured it had something to do with how you can only see what's on the surface, but that there is usually much more to something than meets the eye.

One of the other girls on the trip overheard our conversation and asked if she could join us. I didn't know her at all yet and didn't really want her to hear what I was saying, but Steve told her she could join in anyways. He helped me out and reminded me that her name was Katie.

"It's kind of like when you see a homeless person on the street. It's easy to say they are homeless because they are lazy or a drunk or something like that. But maybe they have some serious mental issues that got them there. There are all sorts of reasons you couldn't possibly understand until you experienced them yourself."

Katie was from Las Vegas. She and her little sister came on this trip together and had both been homeschooled their entire lives. They were raised in a super religious family. I don't know why anyone who is religious would live in a place like Las Vegas. It just doesn't make any sense to me.

"But most bums are still lazy," I said, "You can't forget that."

"I think that's the point she is trying to make Kris," Steve tried to explain, "What you see as someone being lazy is just the surface, the tip of the iceberg, but there is much more to that person and their story than being lazy, and the only way you could ever hope to find any of that out…"

"Is if I ram them with my kayak?" I interrupted, trying to be funny. But neither of them laughed. The conversation was pretty much over after that. I tried to understand what they meant, but I thought that using bums as an example was a bad choice. They are lazy. Everyone knows that.

4 pm: I decided to explore a little on my own before dinner. I am trying to get a better view of the glacier we are next to. To see it from a different perspective.

We were right on the edge between dry land and a glacier field. So I climbed up the hillside a ways to get a better look. It felt like I was on another planet. I was climbing around on this endless slab of rock with little patches of grass and bushes growing out of it. Right next to me was this field of stacked ice that was slowly making its way from the mountains to the sea. You couldn't see it moving, but it was. I felt like an explorer, and could tell that I was the first person in the history of the world to ever set foot at that particular spot.

But I wasn't.

I knew I wasn't when out of the corner of my eye, I saw this piece of toilet paper sticking out of the ground. The closer I looked I realized that this secret spot I had discovered was really just someone else's personal crapper. And the jerk didn't even do it right. The whole thing really bothered me. I finally understood why we didn't bring toilet paper into the back-country. Seeing it there really ruined the whole experience for me, and I began to wonder if I would ever find a place that no one else had set foot on. If that sort of thing was even possible in this day and age.

The whole experience of being next to something so big made me feel small. Insignificant. I returned to camp feeling tired and depressed. But I wasn't gonna share that at the meeting. Not a chance.

DAY TEN:

7 am: This morning we have to pack up camp and get back in our kayaks to go watch the glacier calving. I'm pretty excited and plan on paddling as close as possible.

When we made it to this one section of the glacier, the noise of falling ice was thunderous. It almost seemed like we were too close and I actually felt a little scared after realizing how awesomely powerful nature could be. The sheer size of the ice wall was overwhelming. But the beauty and intricacy of the glacier seemed like a waste as I watched it crack and fracture, only to fall into the water where it would disappear forever.

I still wasn't a big fan of nature, but I was definitely learning a new respect for it. When the really big pieces of ice fell they created waves and a gust of wind. We got so close that if a big enough piece were to fall, we could have been tipped over by the wave it would make.

2 pm: After spending the morning watching the glaciers, we headed back to the Ewok Island. There was a tail wind so I didn't seem to mind the extra distance we had to cover. When we got back Tyson and Andrea asked if anyone wanted to swim in the glacier water. I don't know why, but I was the first one to volunteer.

We could see icebergs floating by as we got ready to jump in. Anxiety filled my body, but in a good way that reminded me I was alive. I hadn't felt like that in a long time. And for the first time I accepted the fact that maybe getting sent on this trip wasn't such a bad thing after all.

Five of us decided to jump in, including Jennifer. She looked so good in her little bikini. A part of me wanted to chicken out but

I knew it was too late for that. So we all counted to three and ran into the water together.

The water was so cold it took my breath away.

I mean it. I really couldn't breathe for a second or two and thought it was all over for me. Everyone was out even quicker than they got in. Except for Tyson and Andrea. They had this game to see who could last the longest. After about a minute and a half Tyson yelped and ran back to shore. I couldn't believe how tough Andrea was.

2:15 pm: My whole body is still stinging from the freezing cold water! Tyson made a big old fire before we jumped in and it feels so good to be warming up by it now. That was hands down the craziest thing I have ever done. But if I had to go back and do it all over again, I guess I would. How weird is that?

I guess it had something to do with the feeling it left me with inside. How I felt completely alive, and I wasn't the only one.

At our meeting a few of the other kids talked about it too. This scrawny kid named Josh told us how he takes all these medications for depression and all sorts of other things his doctor diagnosed him with. How the meds are supposed to help him appreciate things better. But ever since he started taking them he just feels like a zombie all the time. He doesn't get depressed anymore, but he doesn't really feel much of anything. "But today," Josh went on, "Today when I jumped in the glacier water I could actually feel something other than numbness."

The last part sounded kind of funny to me because the water was so cold that it made my body numb as soon as I touched it. Steve pointed out the irony and Josh replied, "That's what was so nice, my body felt numb but my insides didn't. I felt alive inside. I miss that."

A few of us snapped our fingers at Josh for sharing such a private detail about his life. That's what we do at our meetings when someone says something that you like or that you can relate to, you snap to let them know you understand how they feel.

Then Jennifer told us that she took meds too, but that they were the best thing that ever happened to her. She insisted that they saved her life. How before she started taking them she always felt out of control and could never concentrate in school. She said getting good grades that would help her get into an Ivy League school was worth the side effects for her and that she couldn't imagine not taking them. I wondered how else they affected her, what she might be like without them.

Another girl told us that she used to swear by her meds, that they were the only thing that could help her cope with something that happened to her, though she wouldn't go into any details. No one pushed the issue. Hell, she probably didn't get the birthday present she asked for or something. But she did tell us how she asked her parents if she could try taking a "vacation" from the meds for the summer and they said yes. You could tell all this was a surprise to the leaders and they weren't quite sure how to react. Her name was Lucy. She was a real sweet, yet quiet girl. She confessed that she still wasn't sure which way she liked living more, with or without the pills.

The therapists and doctors tried to give me a bunch of meds too, but I couldn't stand it. My parents only agreed to it after the fight, but after the first month I figured out a way to hide them in my mouth without getting caught. It scares the crap out of me to think I'd have to take some pill for the rest of my life. Do they really think I am not capable of being normal on my own? Is my head really that screwed up?

Something about meds just felt wrong to me. Like some people were just looking for a quick fix. Something to keep the rest of us in line. And if our emotions were what needed to be sacrificed for *their*—for society's—convenience, well screw that. The more I thought about it the crazier it seemed. That a doctor could say to a kid that a specific process in their brain wasn't *normal*, but that a magic pill could easily fix the problem, never mind the fact that there would be a ton of side effects in the process. What kind of a fix was that? I bet that fifty years from now people will look back at how much medication used to be prescribed and laugh. Maybe even feel ashamed.

But then again, maybe Jennifer was right. Maybe medication *is* the answer. It just sounds so scary to me. To feel like Josh says he does all the time. I'd rather have the extreme ups and downs over a steady numbness. I just wish the ups came a little more often on their own, that's all.

DAY ELEVEN:

12 pm: We just paddled back to where our van is parked. There were a ton of waterfalls I hadn't really noticed on the way to the Ewok Island, and we were able to get super close to some of them. The mist from the waterfalls was cold but refreshing.

A warm breeze tickled the surface of the water further back away from the waterfalls. There were hundreds of birds, maybe even a thousand that were flying around in circles. It looked like they were playing with each other in the wind. Andrea saw me watching them and explained to me that the birds were using updrafts called thermals to gain height without having to use very much energy. She thought they were either looking for a place to roost or possibly trying to defend themselves from a larger bird of prey by flying close together.

"Safety in numbers," I said, "I think I would rather be the hunter than the prey."

"It must be nice to have the luxury of being able to choose," responded Andrea as she paddled off to help out Josh who was straggling behind.

Josh was kind of a baby, but always trying to impress the rest of the group. He was rarely successful. He was real scrawny and always complaining that things were too tough for him. He was from the east coast, Delaware I think.

Andrea's comment haunted me more than she could have known and I wondered if we really did have a choice. I was certainly trying to act like a predator rather than prey on this trip, and I wondered if any of the other kids knew the half of it.

1:30 pm: Said a quick good bye to the mean kayak lady and just drove back through the long tunnel. Tyson honked the horn the entire time.

I imagined the sound waves creating a rockslide and trapping us, but that never happened. We were all going nuts the whole time, shouting and making the van sway from side to side. The other cars must have thought we were crazy.

2:45 pm: About to stop at a grocery store to resupply before driving to our next campsite halfway between here and another glacier where we start ice climbing the day after tomorrow. Scared about climbing but can't wait to play with the axes.

Before we stopped at the grocery store, we all got in our cook groups and had to plan the meals we were going to make for the next few days. But first we had to run them by Tyson and Andrea. All the food up until now had already been provided. The company Andrea and Tyson worked for still paid for the food, but we were responsible for the shopping from here on out. Andrea tried to give us some advice before letting us loose, but we were all too excited to bother listening.

Go figure, our first experience shopping for food in our cook groups was a complete disaster. Most of the group had never been shopping in a grocery store on their own before. What should have taken a half hour dragged on for almost two. Everyone was getting frustrated. When we finally finished, Andrea could tell the experience nearly destroyed whatever group dynamics had been previously established. I think we were all kind of surprised with how quickly we turned on each other.

We all knew we should have listened to her advice a little better, but no one was going to admit it. I was waiting for her to hold it over us with a typical, "I told ya so." But she never did. Instead, out of nowhere she surprised us by treating everyone to ice cream. I couldn't believe it. It was amazing how such a simple gesture restored our spirits. While we enjoyed our single scoop treats, she casually gave us some pointers for our next shop. This time we were eager to listen.

9 pm: We set up camp and took it easy for the rest of the night. Jennifer was our "Leader-of-the-day" and she made sure our meeting was short and sweet. I liked that it was a quick one. That's how my meeting is gonna be too when they make me be "Leader-of-the-day."

DAY TWELVE:

9 am: Today is a drive day. That means the only thing we are doing all day long is driving to our next campsite. I plan on sleeping most of the time. So does everyone else.

Some of the time though I just pretended to sleep. See, I was in the bench seat up front and Tyson and Andrea talked the whole drive. They talked about all sorts of stuff. I kept waiting for them to talk some smack about us but they never did. The thing about them was, they were pretty funny when they didn't think anyone was listening to them. A couple of times I wanted to join in, but figured that might screw things up, so I kept my mouth shut and listened as long as I could. I eventually nodded off until we hit the dirt road to our campsite.

11 pm: When we finally made it we set up camp at a site along a giant river, and made another huge fire. This time there was no one to stop us, and we stayed up all night hypnotized by the flames, listening to stories from Andrea and Tyson.

After our meeting we talked a lot about religion. Tyson told us that he was an atheist. I heard plenty of kids claim they were atheists back home, though I doubted they really knew what they were talking about. But I could tell that Tyson had put a lot of thought into it. He was the first adult in a position of authority who ever admitted to me that he didn't believe in God. I said I was an atheist too when it was my turn, but the truth is I don't really know what to think. I get nervous thinking about that sort of stuff and usually try to avoid the subject all together, I guess. But I sure as hell wasn't going to admit that to the group.

When it was Matt's turn he confessed almost the exact same feelings that I was too nervous to. I couldn't believe he was willing to admit something like that to everyone else. Andrea thanked him for sharing. I knew she should have been thanking me too. Then she reminded us that it was important to explore the uncertainties that we might be afraid of examining. You know, stuff about both life and what happens after you die. Just thinking about it made me uncomfortable.

I don't think some of the group got what she was talking about. It was clear Jennifer was too busy making judgments about those who said they didn't know what they believed or that they didn't believe in God at all. Jennifer said that she knew there was a God without a doubt, and that she wasn't afraid of dying at all. How is that even possible? Everyone's gotta be a little afraid of dying, right?

Despite Jennifer's comments, Katie's little sister, Sarah, said that she wanted to believe in God, but had doubts on a regular basis. Jeff told us that he was a proud Jew, but didn't think God was real at all. He tried to explain it, but it was over my head.

I couldn't believe how open everyone was about such a controversial topic. We had only known each other for twelve days. I still wasn't saying much during the nightly meetings, though I was beginning to listen more. People were bringing up ideas that I had never even thought about before. They were asking questions that I always wanted to, but thought would make me come off as vulnerable or weak if I did.

Watching everyone else bond during the meetings made me want to join in. Be a part of the group instead of on my own. I felt kind of bad that I still didn't know everyone's name. Sometimes I wondered how I got into the habit of being too cool for everyone else. I knew this was a good group. And I knew a part of me wanted to join in. So why was I trying so hard to distance myself from them? I ended up making a deal with myself that I would at least try to learn everyone's names.

For the rest of the night I listened and enjoyed the fire. I tried to put my hand on Jennifer's leg, but she told me to stop loud enough for the rest of the group to hear. I felt like an idiot and don't think I will be trying that again anytime soon.

DAY THIRTEEN:

10 am: We woke up and walked over to the base of the glacier where we were going to learn how to ice climb for the next week. Met the guides. They seem way cooler than the last one we went kayaking with. Tyson and Andrea showed up looking like cowboys and the guides got a real kick out of it.

What happened was we were all supposed to bring these things called *gaiters* for ice climbing. They go around a person's boots and over their pants and are made out of tough material so that no one tears up their pants with the razor sharp ice cleats that attach to the bottom of our boots for climbing. The cleats are called crampons and they are full of sharp edges. But the two sisters from Vegas, I mean Katie and Sarah, ended up going to this redneck outdoor store for all their gear, and the guy at the shop had no clue what gaiters were so he sold them each a pair of cowboy chaps made out of real rawhide instead.

When we all met up to walk to the glacier and meet the guides, Katie and Sarah saw that they had the wrong gear and got super embarrassed. So what Tyson and Andrea did was traded their gaiters for the girls' chaps. Then they cut holes in these old Mexican blankets that they had and wore them like ponchos. To top it all off they both put on their cowboy hats too.

They looked so goofy and out of place that the ice climbing guides didn't know what to make of it when they saw Andrea and Tyson walking up in head to toe cowboy gear. Before they could ask any questions Tyson asked with astonishment, "Hey wait a minute, where's all the horses at?"

Everyone got a real kick out of it and they kept their outfits on the rest of the day. I would have thought it was all real dumb if I didn't know they were only doing it so that the girls didn't feel self-conscious for having to wear the chaps themselves.

11 am: The guides are teaching us how to climb. We are also learning to belay. That's where you attach yourself to the other end of the rope that someone is climbing on.

See, a climber has to be attached to a rope that goes way up to the top of the ice cliff and then back down to the ground. Someone else is attached to the other end, and as the climber scales the ice, the other person takes in the slack so that if the climber falls, the drop is only a foot or so because the belayer catches the climber with the rope. They use this special piece of gear. A belay device. So really, as a climber, your life is in their hands. You have to trust them.

I was already nervous enough about the climbing part since the ice wall was over fifty feet tall, but the fact I had to trust someone from our group with my life made me downright uncomfortable.

1:15 pm: We practiced how to belay all morning on flat ground at the base of the glacier. Now that lunch is over, it is time to try out what we learned on an actual ice wall.

There was a ton of gear that had to be carried to where we were going to climb. The ice guides asked for volunteers to help, and of course Steve and Allen jumped up first. They tried to carry it all by themselves, which was impossible.

"You two are trying way too hard." I pointed out. Then I turned to Tyson, "You see these suckers, carrying a bunch of crap that's not theirs just to look good for the new guides."

His response was simple, "It looks like they could use an extra hand."

"No thanks, I'm not a kiss-ass. That's not really my style."

Tyson just looked at me, "You are the one who is trying too hard Kris."

Then he grabbed a rope and walked away. I just stood there and watched as everyone else picked up the rest of the climbing gear and headed toward the wall. I waited for Jeff, who was always the last person in line.

"Can you believe that," I asked Jeff, "Him saying that I try too hard. I don't try at all. What the hell is he talking about?"

"He's right."

"What?"

"You do try too hard man, it's obvious."

"I just told you, I don't try at all."

"That's the point Kris. You are trying too hard at not trying. I can see through that, and I'm sure Tyson can too."

I couldn't believe Jeff was taking his side. He went on, "Look Kris, I know you are smart, so why do you always act like you aren't?"

"Whatever man, forget it." I was pissed now.

"Even right now, I know you know what I am talking about. Why are you always trying to be *too cool*?"

"Like you don't?"

He shot back, "Not like you man. You go out of your way to be a dick to the group. But I'm gonna let you in on a little secret. It's not doing what you think it is. People don't think you are cool, they just think you are a jerk."

He went on till I told him to mind his own business or I'd sock him. That shut him up real quick. I lingered behind and was the last one to make it to where we were going to climb.

The frozen cliff looked cold and unforgiving. Like it was gonna be Karma's little helper and put me in my place for what just went down. I didn't even want to give it a chance and tried to think of a good excuse for getting out of having to climb. I told Andrea that I didn't feel well and asked if I could go lay down in my tent.

She finally let me go back to lie down, but only after asking a thousand questions about what was hurting and where. I felt bad for lying to her, and worse for chickening out. So I walked past the campsite and found a place to smoke. I thought it would make me feel better but it didn't. Just kept me distracted for a while, that's all.

It really bothered me what Jeff said, about my style not working and all. I didn't want the others to think I was a jerk. I just wanted them to respect me. I told myself that he was full of crap, but it didn't seem to help much.

That night I skipped dinner and pretended I was out cold when Steve came to get me for the meeting. At first I was proud of myself for getting out of another meeting, but after a while I kind of wished I was there for it. I could kind of hear everyone talking and tried to listen as best as I could from my tent. All I could make out was that they were having a good time, and I had chosen to not be a part of it.

DAY FOURTEEN:

8 am: After breakfast we are going back to the glacier for our first full day of ice climbing.

I was exhausted because I didn't get any sleep. I was so pissed at myself for chickening out. I knew I was going to have to climb today. I wanted to. The biggest problem for me was the trust part. I tried to think of who I had teased the least on the trip so far. I ended up asking Steve to belay me. I also picked him because he was the heaviest kid on the trip. I passed some of my fear off onto him and told him that if he dropped me I would kick his ass with my ice cleats still on.

Tyson overheard and let out his typical chuckle. "You really think fear is the best tool to use to get him to take care of you up there?"

I didn't care much for his chuckle this time and said without thinking, "What the hell else is there?"

Tyson looked disappointed. Hurt almost. I hadn't seen that look in him before and I didn't like it. Then he offered up what he was hoping to hear from me, "How about respect?"

"Last time I checked they both get the same results."

"Fear and respect? Maybe they do," he paused, "in the short run. But which one would you rather have someone use on you?"

"Steve! On-belay?" I ignored Tyson and got ready to climb. I was already nervous enough, the last thing I needed was a life lesson.

9:17 am: I made it to the top my first try.

I did. Kind of. The truth of it was that I fell a couple of times. The first time I knew I was going to fall before it happened and screamed out Steve's name. I should have been embarrassed at what a baby I sounded like, but I was too scared to notice at the time. Fortunately Steve was ready and I only dropped a few inches. Like I said, I fell a few more times, but never gave up, and finally made it to the top my first try. The only other kid to do that was Matt. Ice climbing gets tiring awfully quick when you are learning. That's because most people use their arms too much when they should be trusting their feet more. That's why everyone else gave up before making it to the top their first try. Their arms were too damn sore.

The crazy thing about climbing is that even though I knew Steve would catch me if I fell, I was still scared to death of falling. I think everyone was. You really have to trust the person belaying you, and I have never put much trust in anyone before. Trusting Steve was way harder than the climbing part, but climbing was only possible if I put complete trust in him. Even though I was the one climbing, the sport itself is really all about teamwork.

Steve did a good job when it was his turn to climb, but because he's heavier he got tired pretty quick and quit after his first fall. I was nervous that because he was so much heavier than me he would slingshot me up the face of the ice wall. But it doesn't really work that way. When I was letting him down I was extra careful until the very end. I kept him suspended in mid-air about a foot off the ground for as long as I could, then I let him drop quick to the ground. It was so hilarious, I couldn't stop laughing.

Tyson saw the whole thing and got really pissed off at me. He went off about respect and fear some more, and how he knew that I would have hated it if Steve had done something like that to me.

The worst part about it was that Tyson was right. I would have never forgiven Steve if he did something like that to me. I probably would have never wanted to try climbing again either. Even worse, I began to worry that someone else might do the same thing to me now for payback.

Tyson told me that I wasn't allowed to climb again or belay anyone until after lunch. I hated that he was treating me like a little kid by putting me on time-out, and remembered all of the reasons why I didn't like him. I told him I thought climbing was gay anyways, and then he started lecturing me about replacing the word 'gay' with lame.

"Whatever," was all I could muster up.

He kept preaching on and on about the golden rule like I had heard him do a hundred times. I stopped listening pretty quick. It all seemed rather hypocritical to me coming from him. So I asked him, "So let me get this straight, you call yourself an atheist, right?"

He agreed.

"Well if you don't believe in God then why are you always going on and on about Jesus's golden rule?"

He looked me dead in the eyes and made sure he had my full attention before responding, "You don't need to follow a religion to understand the importance of a rule like that. And do you really think that Jesus was the first person to believe in a concept like that?"

I hated that I couldn't come up with a good response.

After lunch was over Tyson allowed me to climb some more. At first no one wanted to belay me except Paul. But Paul was the last person I was going to trust. Not because of anything I had done to him, but because he was so oblivious about everything. No one had let him belay them yet, and you could tell it was bothering him. He literally went around to every single one of us and asked, but everyone had some sort of excuse for him.

I don't think he began to pick up on it until he asked Lucy, the girl who was taking a vacation from her meds. She's the sweetest, most genuine girl ever and even she turned poor Paul down. When he asked her why not you could tell that she thought about making up some sort of an excuse, but just couldn't do it. She was way too honest for that sort of thing. All she said was, "I'm sorry Paul, but I don't think you can handle the responsibility. I mean... do you even realize that you are stepping on the climbing rope with your crampons right now?"

He hadn't noticed, and looked down while stumbling around on the rope a few more times—just as he had done with the bear poop on our backpack—before stepping off of it completely. But since this time he was wearing razor sharp crampons that were piercing the very rope our lives depended on it had the potential to affect all of us.

Lucy's response was said with the best of intentions, but came off as quite possibly the harshest thing Paul had ever heard in his whole life. It was clear that she didn't mean it to be, at least it was to everyone except for Paul. He just stood there like he had been hit with a ton of bricks.

"Paul," Tyson hollered over as if Paul was in trouble. He had been watching the entire time. Then something weird happened. "Get over here," Tyson went on, "I need someone to belay me on this route."

No one could believe what they heard. Not even Tyson I don't think. The only people that looked more surprised than Paul was Andrea and the two guides. They all gave Tyson a look letting him know that he didn't have to put his own life at risk just for Paul's self-esteem.

But the look on Paul's face was telling Tyson that he did. Hell, this might have been the first time in Paul's weird and wacky life that anyone had ever trusted him with anything. And the fact that Tyson decided to do so with his own life made it all that much more insane.

Tyson looked around at all of us as he went on, "I can't expect anyone to do anything I wouldn't do myself."

I couldn't believe it. No one could. One of the guides told Tyson, "You should have been a General. We could have used more people like you when I was in the army."

"Yeah right," I said, "He'd still lead them into surefire death, only difference is that he'd die first."

Tyson just laughed his usual chuckle, "I've always considered myself a pacifist, but I'll take the compliment. On-belay Paul?"

I had always thought of pacifists as people who didn't understand what bravery was, but this was the bravest thing I had ever seen.

Paul was too busy being Paul to think about such things. "Huh, I mean, sure it is."

Andrea interrupted, "You have to be holding the rope before you can say that, Paul. And you are supposed to say 'belay is on.' Remember?"

"Huh? I mean, oh, yeah. I mean, on-belay... I mean, belay is on."

Then Tyson took one last look at us all standing there, wearing what was supposed to be his fear on our own faces. He smiled. It reeked of nervousness.

"Good luck," Katie shouted for inspiration.

"I don't need luck," he assured her, "I have Paul, and I'd take him over luck any day."

We all kind of figured he was lying through his teeth. All of us except for Paul of course. Paul was on cloud-nine.

We watched as a man who couldn't put faith into a God gave it freely to a socially awkward, inept and oblivious teenage boy. At our nightly meetings Tyson had spoken about his belief that people had a habit of stepping up to the plate when great responsibilities were thrust upon them. I guess this was his attempt to prove it by placing his life into Paul's grimy, sweaty hands.

Despite his verbal vote of confidence in Paul, you could tell Tyson was still nervous as all hell as he climbed the cold and unforgiving wall of ice. A few times he came close to falling, and yelled down to make sure that Paul was paying attention. Andrea had strategically positioned herself next to Paul just-in-case and was keeping a close eye on him. Paul would always respond in a way that was anything but reassuring, and Tyson would force his signature chuckle and push on.

Paul never did drop Tyson. You could tell that the experience was good for both of them. It was obvious why it was for Paul, someone finally believed in him. I felt like crap for giving the rest of the group a reason not to believe in me by dropping Steve. As for Tyson, it reaffirmed his faith in his personal philosophy. I always thought the only thing faith had to do with was religion, but Tyson chose to believe in something he thought was even more important. Himself. And us. And I found it odd that this was the first time in my life that the concept seemed worthwhile to me.

It reminded me that he and Andrea really did mean well. And I couldn't help but start to believe that maybe he knew more than I gave him credit for.

He was still kind of a smart ass though. That night he did almost light the entire campground on fire trying to keep the evening fire going. It rained just before dinner and the wood was too wet to stay lit. So he started pouring small amounts of gas onto the fire. At first he would only pour a capful of gas at a time, but soon grew impatient with that and started pouring gas directly from the metal canister it was in. Sure enough, the flame followed the stream up and went right into the bottle.

I always heard that a stunt like that would cause the fuel bottle to explode. Tyson must have heard the same thing because for a split second, it looked like he was going to throw the bottle.

That would have been very bad.

We were all sitting around the fire trying to warm up and trees waited to receive the bottle in every direction. If he had thrown it, everything could have gone up in flames. But the bottle still hadn't exploded so he held tight. There was, however, a steady flame coming out of the bottle's lid.

Tyson attempted to blow the flame out, but in doing so managed to ignite more of the gas, resulting in a temporarily larger flame. Finally he put his arm directly on top of the bottle's opening and the lack of oxygen suffocated the flame. The whole thing happened so quick no one knew how to react. And then Tyson gave his now legendary chuckle. It was contagious and we all joined in with chuckles of our own. Chuckles that were saying the same thing his was. Chuckles that were saying, "I can't believe how calm we all are considering we almost died just now."

He managed to repeat this process three more times before finally calling it a night. By the end, we were egging him on for an encore. I don't know why he kept pushing it. Maybe he felt invincible after surviving his climb with Paul belaying him. Or maybe the confidence needed to perform his new *trick* was fueled by his new understanding of how the flame itself worked. But what really amazed me, scared me actually, was how quickly our minds were able to transform such a dangerous behavior into a form of entertainment. We could have been seriously injured. And we all understood that the first time he did it. So how did our legitimate fear extinguish so quickly in the name of a good time? The craziest part to me was, this sort of thing was probably happening everywhere on a daily basis without anyone ever realizing it.

DAY FIFTEEN:

10 am: Another day of ice climbing. I am becoming less scared of falling and beginning to trust the people belaying me more and more. And because of it I am taking more chances and getting much better at climbing.

Steve wouldn't let me belay him when I asked at the beginning of the day. I wanted to argue with him about it, and make him trust me. But I realized that wouldn't really be him trusting me at all. It was more along the lines of the whole fear vs. respect thing Tyson was so big on. So I let it go, and tried to prove to him that I was trustworthy by belaying the rest of the group. I have to admit that it felt pretty good knowing that most of them were willing to trust me.

All morning I couldn't stop thinking about how Tyson almost started a forest fire the night before, and how quickly we were able to change our perceptions. What was scary one moment transformed into the norm the next. I wasn't sure if it was a good or bad thing, but I tried to relate it to my fear of falling. I tried to alter my perspective and focus on the entertainment that climbing brought rather than the fear it was able to produce. This was easier said than done, but made all the difference when I was able to do so effectively.

Climbing was much easier once I was comfortable with falling. I improved tremendously and everyone seemed to notice. Even one of the ice guides said something to me. Tyson asked me what my secret was. I told him about how I used the incident with the fire as an example to learn from and he gave me a look. It was a good look. One that showed he was impressed. He chuckled softer than usual and said, "It is a wise person who can learn from the most unlikely of experiences."

I understood what he meant.

Then he added, "Just be sure not to mistake the very real dangers in life with your own illusions of fear. That's how people get themselves into trouble."

"Huh?" Just like that he was losing me again.

He began to climb as he mumbled, "Perceived risks versus real risks."

And that was that. Just when I thought I understood, he had to go taking it to another level. I watched him scale the wall of ice with ease and confidence. He kept on saying it over and over again in a calm and neutral voice, "Perceived risks versus real risks, perceived risk, real risk," and I couldn't tell if he was talking to himself or me.

12:30 pm: For the first part of the day, rather than clinging on for dear life when I thought I might fall, I tried to allow myself to calmly fall back and let the rope be what it was: a safety net. The more I did this the more comfortable I became. After lunch I am going to try not to think about falling at all.

During lunch we all sat in a circle and boasted about what good ice climbers we had become. Everyone that is, except for Matt. He was good at it, like he was good at everything, but he didn't seem to enjoy it and never tried any of the harder routes.

Paul was the last one to arrive to the circle, leaving a dilemma. The circle had been completed, save for a spot occupied by a small bush. Without thinking twice, Paul plopped himself down right on top of it. It seemed to swallow him whole and the ice guides began to giggle. This was new behavior for them, while the rest of us were pretty used to it by now. They couldn't stop laughing and pretty soon we were all cracking up, including Paul.

There is something about Paul. A draw that I can't quite explain. In a way he reminds me of a baby trapped in the body of a teenager. His innocence to the world around him is almost unbelievable. I imagine I will recognize his name in the Darwin Awards for *Most Bizarre Accidental Death* one day. It's not that he doesn't know any better. I think he does. There's not much to know really. He just can't help himself. He is that one piece of the puzzle, the solid colored seven sided squiggly one that couldn't possibly match up anywhere. That's Paul. I can't help but find myself intrigued by him, because as strange as he is, the puzzle wouldn't be complete without him.

All during lunch he was going on and on about how he was going to hose down the side of his parents' house next winter and turn it into an ice wall of his very own. We could all picture him attempting this as he described his plan one detail at a time, forgetting to take into account things like the depth of ice and his parents' permission. I imagined him miraculously making it work somehow, and him driving one ice axe at a time through the thin layer of ice he would manage to create and into the wood on the side of his house. I could see it all so clearly, his mom curling her hair as she looked out the second story window, only to see Paul's goofy smile and an ice axe crushing through the thin veneer of ice, shattering both the window as well as her hopes of him ever being a normal person.

Maybe that's the draw with someone like Paul. I know a lot of normal people. They have this habit of being dull and boring. I don't think anyone would ever accuse Paul of such things. His innocence complemented by his curiosity was far too compelling for labels like that. And so we listened with pleasure as he went on and on, till it was time to get back to the frozen walls.

Before we were done for the day I asked Steve for one more chance. He must have been able to tell that it was really bothering me because this time he agreed. But he made sure I knew that if I messed with him he would never trust me again. For some reason, because of the way that he said it I couldn't stop thinking about screwing with him the whole time he was climbing. Part of me really wanted to. I don't know why, I just couldn't help it.

But I didn't. A week ago I am sure that I would have. But I was beginning to understand something. That feeling, knowing that someone trusts you, lasts a lot longer than the feeling you get when you mess with somebody. It is a good feeling. A feeling I could see myself getting used to one day, after I could move away and really start over.

10 pm: Katie, Sarah, and Allen made us an Asian noodle dish for dinner tonight. It was hands down the best meal we have had on the trip so far. Even better than the pizza from town. So far this has been my favorite day. And I was two peoples 'Hero-of-the-day' because of how well I did climbing. But the craziest part was that Matt announced at the meeting that I was going to be tomorrow's Leader-of-the-day. I wasn't very excited about it at first, but have decided to give it my best.

Each night the Leader-of-the-day gets to pick who is going to be the next one. Some of the more natural leaders in the group have already been picked a couple of times. I was kind of hoping that I could get through the whole summer without being picked at all, but it did feel kind of good when Matt said my name. Everyone else has already done it at least once, and I know I can do better than some of the others.

After our meeting, I decided to hang out by the fire for a while. An hour or so passed, and then it was just me, Lucy and Katie. I mostly just played with the fire while they talked. They'd become very close friends by now. They asked me questions here and there, and I got a kick out of the stuff they liked to talk about.

Katie had grown up with religion all her life, and I always thought of her as kind of a closed minded person. But she was confiding in us, Lucy mostly, that she started having doubts about the church a few years back. Lucy was just the opposite, and had recently attached herself to some fancy church back home.

Lucy grew up in Texas, but her family moved out to Colorado a few years back. She said she liked Colorado a whole lot more. I asked her why and she thought about it for a long time with a look of pain on her face before finally saying, "I just feel safer there."

I left it at that and started giving Katie a hard time about being religious and growing up in Vegas. I imagined that everyone back home gave her a hard time too. Probably one of the reasons she and her sister were homeschooled. Katie had that religious kind of look to her. I don't know how to describe it. She wasn't ugly or anything. But she wasn't pretty either. Just kind of plain looking. I pictured her living like the Amish do, or something like that back home.

I was trying to talk her into giving me a backrub, but she wasn't having any of it. I wouldn't hook up with her or anything like that, but I figured I could at least get a back rub out of her.

I would hook up with Lucy though. Like I said before, Lucy was quite possibly the nicest person I had ever met. I imagined that a girl like that would balance out someone like me. She seemed so open, as if she had nothing to hide. And she was cute too. Her hair was long and dark, and she still had dimples. But I didn't have the balls to ask her for a backrub. She probably would have done it, because she was so nice and all, but I still couldn't ask. In truth, I only asked Katie because I kind of already knew she would say no. I don't know why, but I do things like that all the time back home. You know, pass on the sure thing and then set myself up for failure. I don't know why though. I really don't.

Eventually they left for their tents, but before going, they told me that they were glad that I stayed and hung out with them. Lucy told me that I should open up more with the group; that I would get more out of the trip if I did so. I started to say something smooth, but stopped and told her I would try.

All in all, it wasn't a bad day. Each day actually feels like it has been better than the last. In a way, I am kind of glad I got sent on this trip.

I ended staying up way too late by the fire. The freedom to do so felt good. But it made me feel lonely too. So I went back to the tent for some company from Jeff and Steve. Of course, they were both dead asleep. Steve was snoring louder than usual, so I elbowed him in the ribs. It did the trick for a while, long enough for me to fall asleep anyways.

DAY SIXTEEN:

6 am: Woke up extra early this morning. There are a lot of responsibilities to being the Leader-of-the-day. I am in charge of waking everyone up and making sure the cook crew doesn't lag with the breakfast. And I really want to do a good job. Well, it's time to wake everyone else up so here goes nothing. Excited. And a little nervous too, I guess.

Things didn't exactly start off so well. Lyle was part of the cook crew whose turn it was to make breakfast and he wouldn't get out of his tent. It pissed me off because I truly wanted to do a good job as the Leader-of-the-day. Not that I was trying to prove anything to Andrea or Tyson, I just wanted to. For me. But Lyle was making things as difficult as he could. I figured that it probably had something to do with the fact that I was the one Tyson asked to help find the trail back when Lyle was the Leader-of-the-day and this was his way of getting back at me. What a bitter brat.

All morning long he was getting on my nerves, and I could tell he was doing it on purpose. I hate kids like that. The worst part was, the more I told him what he had to do, the more he refused to do anything at all. He was only being like that because Tyson and Andrea had to go talk to the rangers about something and told us they would be gone for a half hour or so. He wasn't just pissing me off either. Everyone was annoyed by him and the crap that he had been pulling since the trip started.

When he refused to clean the dishes from breakfast I had enough. I was trying, but my patience was almost gone, "It's your crew's turn Lyle. No one else complains, now just do it."

"Quit bossing me around Kris. I don't take orders from trash like you." He tried to sound so superior the way he said it, but really he just sounded like a douche bag.

Then Jeff chimed in, "Do it or Kris will make you do it," and the way he said it I felt like Jeff was trying to orchestrate a fight or something, which I really didn't want to be a part of. But that was the energy that was building and it was getting the best of me. I kept waiting for something to change. The leaders to come back or one of the girls to tell us both to knock it off, but instead the tension kept growing, fueled by Jeff and soon Josh too. The worst part of it was that Andrea and Tyson specifically left me in charge while they were gone. So the last thing I wanted was any trouble, especially not a fight.

But Lyle wasn't backing down. I didn't know what the best way to handle the situation was, so I went with the only way I ever knew. Intimidation. I figured one serious threat would be enough to scare him off. So with a real serious look in my eyes I got right up in his face. I told him, "Don't push my buttons Lyle. You don't know what I am capable of."

I didn't want to fight. Just scare him enough to make him do what he was supposed to be doing. That's how it worked back home. I could tell he was scared because he'd heard what a good fighter I was, and I was trying to use my reputation to my advantage. But something went wrong. He didn't back down. He should have. I was bigger than him, and I was sure he'd never been in a fight in his life. But he just stood there. Waiting for me to do something.

Maybe it was because the rest of the group was egging both of us on, but neither of us seemed like we were going to back down. My heart was racing by now, and in a last ditch effort I tried one last time to scare him into submission. "Turn around and finish the goddamn dishes Lyle," then I whispered just loud enough for everyone to hear, "you little faggot."

I watched the tears well up in his eyes. His fear turned to rage, and I knew I failed. The only thing I managed to achieve was the ability to become what I hated. A bully.

And then it hit me. His fist that is. I should have seen it coming but I was too busy psychoanalyzing myself. He missed my face and hit me on my shoulder. That should have been my chance, but before I could react, he hit me again with his other fist right in my chest. That's the one that knocked the wind out of me.

I could hear the rest of the kids yelling in the background, but I couldn't distinguish any of their voices or what they were saying. I always dreamed that I would be able to hear all of the words of encouragement in a fight where people wanted *me* to be winning. So that their voices would help fuel me with power, or something like that. But in reality it was the same as all the other times. Nothing could be cyphered, and the noise only got in the way. Only made things worse.

I swung and I kicked with desperation, but I couldn't land a goddamn thing. Lyle wasn't very accurate either, but there was no doubt for a second who was winning. Even I knew that, and when you are in a fight and know the real score it means you're in serious trouble. Knowing you are losing messes with your head, while at the same time strengthening your opponent. Pretty soon we were just wrestling around on the ground. I tried to smear a bunch of dirt in his face out of desperation, but he beat me to it. Then he was finally able to make a solid connection. His fist met my nose and then it was done. Blood streamed out and all the noises stopped. I foolishly thought it was a sign of solidarity for me, but quickly understood the real reason.

Tyson and Andrea had returned and were running towards us.

I knew exactly what this meant. For one thing, whatever perceptions there were by the group of me being tough were just thrown out the window. Hell, maybe that was a good thing. Maybe I could finally stop pretending to be someone I wasn't, they must've figured out by now that I was never a big fighter back home if I couldn't even beat up a kid like Lyle.

Not that it really mattered, because what the fight really meant was that I was going to be sent home. Only it won't be home this time. This time it would be a done deal. A no-brainer for the courts. No more hopes of *rehabilitation*. This time I would be going away. I could be sure of that.

There was no need to put on an act anymore. There were really no more choices; only one thing left to do. The thing I was raised to avoid at all costs, especially in front of others. Something I'd wanted to do for so long. Needed to really.

The tears welling up on the inside were soon overflowing from the internal walls that I managed to build up for protection over the years. Walls that once seemed impenetrable and endless in height had finally met their match. I could feel them cracking, and soon the walls began to crumble, and when they finally collapsed, a flood of tears surged from hidden chambers in my head out into the open for all to witness.

I would say that it felt good to cry, but it wasn't really like that. All I can say is that it was needed. Nothing had ever been needed so bad in my whole goddamn life. And I wondered why I was raised to believe that such an important thing was so unacceptable, so un-manly. The world was hard enough already. Why we added such unnatural rules in hopes of hiding away our emotions was beyond me.

Andrea and Tyson gathered everyone around and began talking about what this meant for the group dynamic and all that sort of stuff. I couldn't stop crying.

Why? There were a million reasons to cry, but most of all I was crying because it was no use anymore. The group knew I had been lying to them so I decided to come clean. They all kept asking the same question anyways, the one I hoped I'd never have to explain again.

"Wait a second," Matt said when Andrea opened up the discussion to everyone, "How did you get in trouble for fighting back home? I mean, Lyle has never been in a fight in his life, he's a little smaller than you, and he just kicked your ass. I don't get it."

Andrea tried to change the subject, but I stopped her. I knew I had to tell them.

"There's something I gotta tell you guys, but you're not going to like it. But please, please believe me when I tell you that I'm not proud of it at all."

"Proud of what?" Jennifer asked, "What did you do back home to get sent up here anyways?"

"Well first of all, it's not very normal for a kid to get sent away to a fancy trip like this when they get in a fight where I come from."

Jeff kidded, "Don't worry, I don't think that's normal anywhere."

Then Katie added, "Yeah, I don't think that really made sense to any of us, to be honest."

"So what happened then?" asked Lucy.

"Well, you know how I said that I was pretty tough back home?" I took a deep breath, "It's actually the complete opposite."

"What do you mean?" Steve asked with total confusion— almost disbelief—painted across his face.

So I explained it to them and once I started there was no stopping, "Well, I've been bullied pretty much every day of my life ever since junior high back home. A lot of people picked on me, but there's one kid, his name is Cody, who's really had it out for me the worst. He's picked on me since the 7th grade. I hate him. I used to have dreams where I got to bully him around, where I would watch him die. I know that sounds messed up, but you don't know what it is like to be picked on day in and day out for years and years. So I did the same thing to kids weaker than me. Nothing too crazy though."

As soon as I said the part about watching him die I could see that I was losing some of them because they thought something was wrong with me, but I was past worrying what other people thought. I just wanted to say how I really felt for once in my life. Besides, I figured lots of people had messed up dreams; the only difference was that they didn't admit them to other people, but that didn't make them any less real.

"Anyways," I went on, "Cody had just 'spilled' a full cup of soda, a big 20 oz. one, all over me and then punched me right in the gut because some of it splashed onto him. There were lots of other kids around. They were all just laughing, reinforcing to Cody that his behavior was acceptable. When the principal showed up and saw me, he just shook his head, like he was disappointed that he had to deal with me one more time. When he asked what happened, no one in the crowd said a thing.

"I didn't either. I mean, this sort of thing happened all the time. So I just sat there while the principal told me that I needed to stand up for myself, as if I never heard or thought about that before. Like there was actually a simple solution to such a complicated problem."

Everyone in the group was silent. I wasn't trying to make them feel sorry for me, I just wanted them to understand.

"Anyways, that was the day that I decided I was going to hang myself in the closet of my room."

Lucy began to cry.

I didn't stop. I couldn't now, "I wrote out a note that afternoon in class for my parents, telling them that I loved them and all. But when I was walking home from school that day, Cody's kid brother just happened to be walking down the same alley at the same time. You see, I always go through this one alley to avoid where some of the kids hang out after school. Anyways, I was walking down the alley and ran into Cody's little brother. He's a nice enough kid, only in fifth grade. Anyways..."

But I didn't want to go on, I was starting to feel sick in my stomach just thinking about it.

"What? What happened next?" Katie asked. But I could tell from the way they were all looking at me that they already knew what happened next.

I took another deep breath, and tried not to relive what I was describing, "I saw Cody's little brother, all alone in the alley, and I just started hitting him. Something snapped inside of me. I had lost all hope and became a monster. I don't really remember that much once I started in on him. Just that the blood was really flying up in the air, like it does in the movies. I always thought that was so fake, but I can still see it so clearly, that poor kids blood splashing all over the place."

There were a few shrieks while I was explaining all this.

"But why? Why would you hit that poor little kid?" Sarah was appalled as she asked, fearful of any answer I could give.

"I don't know. I wish I knew why it happened like that, why I did to him what others had done to me, but I don't. That's what all the shrinks were trying to figure out too. All I can say is that once I started it was as if I was hitting every bastard who ever picked on me. They were the ones I thought I was hurting when I kept bashing that poor kid's face into the ground."

Some of the girls started to cry. Most of them looked disgusted with me. I was disgusted with myself too, but I didn't expect anyone to believe that. Tears were now pouring from my eyes again, and everything was blurry. Everything except for the memories that I wished would go away.

"Did you, did you… kill him?" Steve asked, and he was afraid of the answer too.

"No, thank God. Almost though. That's what the doctors said. He was in the hospital for a long time. The truth is I felt really sorry for that kid and what I did to him. I felt terrible. I still do. I think about it all of the time. It haunts my dreams. I really don't like violence. I'm not a fighter at all. And I don't really want to be either. But they told me this trip was a chance to reinvent myself and I just figured that was the only way you guys would leave me alone."

It was quiet for a long time, which was the worst. Finally Sarah broke the silence. "So what happened to you next?"

"Someone called the cops. In a way I am glad. I never even made it home that day. Then, well, no one really knew what to do with me. Especially after they found the note to my parents in my backpack. A lot of people wanted me to go to jail. My parents didn't really know what to do, and they couldn't afford a lawyer. But there was this one teacher at school. She fought to make sure that I didn't go to jail and helped find the program that sent me up here and paid for this trip. But a lot of people back home are convinced that I am some psycho who might go crazy one day. That I am no different than the types of kids who shoot up schools."

"Are you?" Jennifer was cold when she said it, and I didn't know what to say.

"I never wanted to do anything like that, I just wanted to be left alone."

"I think that's all some of those kids wanted too." It was the first time either of the leaders had said anything, and the way that Andrea said it I could tell that she understood.

"That's what the quacks said too," I explained, "That's why I had to talk to so many shrinks and doctors. That's why they gave me meds. And that's why I got sent up here. This was supposed to be a fresh start, a new beginning. That's why no one was supposed to know anything about the details of what happened. But I guess I ruined all this now too. Which really sucks because I was finally starting to enjoy myself a little. First time in years, actually."

I could tell that there wasn't much sympathy, despite the sincerity of what I was saying. But I kept going. The only thing I had left was the truth, and I wanted to get it all out. "I hate that I ruined this. I hate that I ruined that kid's face. I hate who I have become. And I hate the reality that intimidation gets results. That's what I was trying to do with Lyle. I didn't want to fight him, I just wanted to get him to do something."

"Do you really think intimidation was the best way?" Tyson asked.

"It's the only way I've ever known. I know what you are going to say. About that whole fear versus respect thing. But I couldn't do it. Not with Lyle. He was supposed to respect *me*. I was the Leader-of-the-day."

But I knew it didn't really work like that. That the only person I really had to blame was myself. I told the group I understood that, and that I knew I was a monster for what I had done, and the tears returned as I buried my head back into my knees, knowing that even the truth wasn't enough for them to understand. And then the strangest thing happened. I felt somebody's arm wrap itself around me.

The rest of the day was pretty much shot.

Tyson and Andrea spent most of the time talking with the rest of the group. Then to everyone individually while the others got to climb. They called their boss to tell him about what happened, and then talked to me and Lyle on our own a bunch more.

I figured that the leaders would send me home. They certainly could if they wanted to. I kept on thinking about everything that had happened on the trip so far. I didn't want to forget all of the experiences.

The thing that bothered me most was how much I had fought having any fun the whole time I was in Alaska. I went out of my way not to give it a chance from the beginning. I wished I could have been like Allen and Steve, gung-ho about everything. When Andrea asked me what my biggest regret was about the trip, that was what I told her. I think it took her by surprise a little. She was probably expecting the obvious, that I was sorry for fighting with Lyle. Which I was. But not nearly as much as I was for not making the most of the opportunity I had been given. The one I had just pissed away.

I don't know why it took so much to learn such a simple lesson. But at least I learned it. And that fact gave me some hope, that there was a chance I could be *rehabilitated* after all. Whatever that was supposed to mean anyways.

Andrea and Tyson sat for a long time without saying anything before they had us all meet up in a group. First they talked to everyone else except for me and Lyle. Finally, they called the two of us over.

The whole thing was pretty nerve-racking, but within a few minutes, it was clear that we were both going to stay on the trip. "But there are some conditions," Andrea explained, "And they are not negotiable."

I agreed before hearing them and Tyson told me to listen to them first. That I might not want to agree after I heard them. So I listened.

Andrea started, "Apparently the whole point of you coming on this trip was for you to have a fresh start, but you ensured the impossibility of that happening with your attitude, as well as your lack of honesty, to us as well as yourself. So if you are to stay, this must change."

Then Tyson stepped in, "Today was a big day. Bigger than you can understand now. But I believe that today is the closest opportunity to a fresh start you've had. Ever perhaps. And we feel like it would be a shame to waste such an opportunity, in the same way that you did with the first part of this trip."

Andrea jumped back in, "But in light of the honesty that you displayed with us today, we were finally able to see a glimpse of who you really are. And none of us, Kris, think you are a monster."

I wondered if that was really the case. I figured at least one of them had to think I was. But their faces showed me that maybe it was possible. Then, one by one, everyone gave a condition for me to agree to. Most of them revolved around me being honest and promising to give things a chance. To avoid being negative and instead focus on the positive. Even Paul had thoughtful things to say, although he eventually got onto a tangent about me sharing my trail mix with him.

The whole thing would have probably come off as cheesy to an outsider, but I heard every word each one of them said. I knew I was capable of everything they were asking, even though I never really gave an honest attempt towards such simple requests before.

I also knew they were right, and I understood this was the only way to really have a fresh start: by being honest with myself. You can't just pretend to be somebody you're not. I mean, you can, but then you are always putting on a show. You never get to feel comfortable. And that's no good at all. So I agreed to all of it, and I meant it too.

By the time we were done, it was late and Andrea asked everyone to go to their tents. I couldn't sleep for a long time. I decided not to write about the fight with Lyle in my journal. I doubted my proby would understand how, in a way, it was kind of a blessing in disguise. At least that's what Andrea called it. I figured I'd wait and tell him in person. You know, face to face. But I was gonna try to be more positive, and I thought a solid entry was as good a place to start as any.

10:15 pm: All I can say is being the Leader-of-the-day sure didn't turn out the way I expected. It was a long, tough day. One of the hardest of my life. But I learned a lot, and feel grateful for the opportunity I have been given. And starting right now I have decided to focus on the positive and make the most out of the rest of this trip. Don't worry, I finally get it. Better late than never, right?

I was awake for a long time, restless in my sleeping bag. I couldn't stop thinking about the opportunity I had been given. I was terrified I would fail. But then I wondered, was it really possible to fail at being yourself?

DAY SEVENTEEN:

7 am: Woke up early on my own again even though I didn't sleep much last night. We still have three more days of ice climbing, and although I want to make the most out of the time, I don't feel much like climbing at the moment. I guess I just have a lot on my mind.

I spent most of the morning worrying about how it was going to be with everyone. I over-read into every glance that came my way. I was sure they were gonna change their minds about letting me stay. So I mostly just tried to fly under the radar.

The entire morning passed and I still hadn't climbed. No one asked me to belay them either. Everyone just kind of let me be. At lunch Tyson asked if I was planning to climb at all.

"I'm just trying to figure things out mostly. Didn't want to bother asking anyone to belay me."

"What about asking Lyle?"

"Uh, no thanks. I know I need to be more open but that seems like a little much right now."

"Fair enough, well how about I belay you then?"

"It's not like I'm Paul or anything. Am I?"

Tyson just chuckled, "No. No, not at all. There can only be one Paul. And that's Paul, right there."

He was trying to be funny but I wasn't really in the mood. Then he went on, "Look Kris, I think it is great that you're trying to process everything from yesterday, but it might be good to get your mind off it for a little bit too. And I guarantee that the route the guides are about to set up would take all of your

86

concentration." Then he added, "Besides, I think you are the only one in the group who can make it to the top."

That was enough to perk my interest.

12:45 pm: While we are finishing our lunch the guides are setting up the hardest route yet. It looks pretty challenging.

Everyone wanted to climb the new route. After they all had a turn, I decided to give it a go. When I touched the anchor at the top of the ice wall I could hear a rumble from down below. But unlike the fight, everyone's voices were crystal clear now. I could hear every word, and they were all positive. I think some of them, mostly Steve and Allen, were more excited than I was and it felt good to hear people cheering for me. I couldn't remember the last time that happened.

Everyone congratulated me once I was lowered back to the ground. Then Tyson asked if I would belay him. He asked for advice at a couple of the hard parts of the climb. It turns out I am kind of a pretty good coach at ice climbing. At least that's what Tyson told me afterwards.

3:30 pm: Tyson and I were the only ones who made it to the top.

That night at our meeting I was still pretty quiet. I could tell some of the group was still unsure about me. But I was also a couple of people's Hero-of-the-day. The one that meant the most though was from Tyson. I told him he was my hero too for talking me into trying that super hard climb. Right before the meeting ended I asked if I could add one more thing. I told the group that they were all my heroes for giving me a second chance. I think it came off as kind of cheesy, but at least I tried. Only time will tell if they really are willing to give me another chance.

DAY EIGHTEEN:

8 am: Still feeling good this morning from yesterday's climb. Can't wait to do some more.

I was super pumped for climbing and couldn't wait to get back to the glacier walls. A couple of the girls were lagging getting ready and I kind of snapped at them. I didn't mean to, but dropping old habits can be hard.

Katie's little sister Sarah called me out right away, "Remember what you promised to work on Kris?"

"Yeah."

She calmly added, "Then try to be a little more patient."

"I am, I just…"

"Then try a little harder," she snapped.

Normally getting called out like that would bother me, but I knew Sarah was just trying to help. So I bit my tongue and waited. By the time everyone else was ready I was already carrying most of the group gear. I started walking until Tyson caught up and stopped me. "Looks like a lot of stuff for one person to be carrying. Why don't you let some of the others give you a hand."

"It's cool," I replied while I tried to make a weight adjustment, "I got it."

"Okay, this just doesn't really seem like it's your style."

"Huh?"

"You know, from the other day…"

"Oh yeah, I get it. That was the old me. This is the new me though. I got it."

"I guess what I am saying is don't try so hard."

"Huh?" I didn't get it. What did he want from me? I got crap when I didn't carry anything, and now I was getting crap for carrying too much.

"Just be yourself Kris. You don't need to make up for the past, just be yourself."

We were a ways ahead of the rest of the group so I set down the gear and looked around. I thought about it for a while and finally confessed, "I am still trying to figure out who that is."

Tyson just stood there. I could tell he was holding back his stupid chuckle. Eventually he offered up, "That's alright, I am still trying to figure out exactly who I am sometimes too."

I wanted to get into it more but the rest of the group had almost caught up to us. I asked Matt if he would give me a hand and he took half of what I was carrying. Tyson gave a look of approval and we made our way into the glacier field.

9:15 am: Today is the deepest we've been into the glacier. We stopped in a spot where we are surrounded on all sides by tall, thick walls of blue. It is kind of eerie.

Everyone was improving at climbing and I belayed as many people as possible without making it look like I was trying too hard. I mainly just wanted to show everyone that I could be a team player. It seemed to work and I had my first conversation with Lucy and Katie since the fight. We mostly talked about how claustrophobic it was with ice all around us. I mostly listened.

11 am: So, out of nowhere one of the guides just asked me if I want to try to lead my first ever sport route. I am full of emotion. ~~Mostly scared~~. Mostly excited. But scared too.

89

Lead climbing means that there is no rope above you. See, one of the guides went first and put a bunch of ice screws into the ice every five feet or so, all the way to the top. Then they set up an anchor at the top of the wall. But after they were lowered back to the ground, they pulled the rope through the anchor. I watched in silence as the rope fell back down to us at the bottom of the wall. It was a long, long fall.

"Your turn," the guide said to me with a smile.

I smiled back. Then I just stood there. As if I didn't know what she was talking about.

"Now remember, each time you come to one of the ice screws you are going to take one of your quick-draws that is already attached to your rope and secure it to the end of the screw."

The way it works is that the rope is attached to me and as I climb I have to keep attaching it to the different ice screws with the quick-draws. A quick-draw is two carabiners attached to a piece of webbing. One of the carabiners clips into the ice screw and the other clips around the rope. That way if I fall, I only fall the distance to the next ice screw below me plus however high I am above it. So if I am twenty feet up on the wall and fall two feet above the last ice screw I attached myself to, then I would fall for four feet before the rope got tight between me and the belayer. So I'd still be sixteen feet off the ground. It was the first time in my life that I ever paid attention to a math lesson. It sounds crazy explaining it but it really wasn't that bad. And besides, they only asked me because they were confident that I wouldn't fall.

So I took a deep breath and dug my axes into the ice. The first ten feet were the worst. But once I clipped into the second ice screw I kind of got into a groove. I was in the zone and I felt like nothing could stop me.

When I returned to the ground everyone ran up and dog piled on top of me.

"Be careful of his ice axes! Watch your crampons!" Andrea almost had a heart attack watching us roll around in the ice with all that sharp metal attached to us, but no one got hurt.

11:20 am: Still alive! I made it to the top without any falls. I couldn't believe it. At first I thought for sure I was going to fall, but once I started climbing something changed. Falling wasn't even an option. I had to trust myself instead of the rope. It was scarier, but it also made me stay more focused. In fact, I'd say it was the scariest thing I have ever done by choice. I feel on top of the world.

I didn't even let it bother me when I overheard Lyle remind Jennifer, "It was an easy route anyways."

He was right, but I didn't care. It was still a big deal and everyone else knew it too. I tried to focus on that instead of letting Lyle bring me down. And for the most part, it worked.

DAY NINETEEN:

9 am: Today is our last day with our ice guides. Instead of climbing, we are doing a Tyrolean traverse. That's where a rope is set up from one peak to another and you have to pull yourself across it. Ours is across a crevasse that's over 100 feet deep!

The plan was that we would go one at a time and would be clipped onto the rope with a harness. I knew it was safe, but it still looked super scary. Way worse than climbing. I could tell some of the girls didn't want to do it at all. I still felt awkward about the day of the fight and was trying extra hard to be nice to everyone. And for the most part, it seemed like everyone was giving me an honest chance.

So I told the girls that I was scared too, hoping to make them feel better. They were shocked I admitted that I was afraid and it kind of bothered me that they thought I was a chicken. Without thinking I added, "We all should be, someone's probably gonna die up there."

Like I said, old habits die hard. I had been fronting for so long that sometimes I didn't even realize I was doing it. Andrea was quick to call me out though. She pulled me aside, "Kris, why would you even say something like that?"

"I don't know, it just kind of came out." I thought about it, and then added, "I know it's not right but it is probably because I am scared too. Really."

"Well scaring them isn't going to make it any less scary for you."

She could tell that I got it and was ready to leave it at that, but then I asked her a favor. "Will you keep calling me out when you catch me saying stuff like that?"

She looked surprised, but assured me she would. She even said she would try to pull me aside to make sure not to embarrass me.

"That's okay," I replied, "You can call me out in front of the others. Well, actually…" I wasn't sure if I really wanted that. Finally I added, "Just do whatever you think is best."

"I will Kris, now go get ready for the traverse."

2:30 pm: Right before I went one of the guides told me not to look down if I was scared. That it would only make it worse. I wish he hadn't said that because it made me feel like I had to look down over the highest point to overcome my fear. And he was right, it did make it seem way worse than it actually was. The white ice turned to blue, blue into black. The hole seemed endless. Time stood still. I felt paralyzed. Katie yelled for me to keep going and I finally regained focus. I told myself this was only a perceived risk and pulled my way across. I was so glad to make it to the other side.

Although it took a while, everyone made it across to the other side. We relaxed for the rest of the day. I was starving and couldn't wait for dinner. Grilled cheese sandwiches never tasted so good.

9pm: The guides joined us this evening for our meeting and we said our goodbyes. They handed out awards too. Paul got one for most improved belayer and I got one for best climber. It was a good way to end the most challenging part of the trip so far.

DAY TWENTY:

9 am: This morning we gotta head back into Anchorage for laundry, showers, and supplies for the next week.

Our first stop was to wash our clothes. It took hours but we relaxed and goofed around. Jeff got stuck in one of the dryers. It was pretty damn funny. Next it was time to get clean. We hadn't showered since just after the backpack. I know that it sounds pretty gross, but we were all getting pretty used to it. The only one who ever really smelled bad was Paul.

He'd worn the same green sweatshirt the entire trip. The sleeves doubled as his primary napkin. They were sticky. Stiff. Even after the Laundromat it still looked dirty. He also had this red and black plaid beanie with him at all times. He said it was his dad's favorite hunting beanie and that he took it without asking right before he left. I only mention it because he was so proud of the fact. But I have seen him wipe his runny nose on the inside of it multiple times. Then he just puts it right back on his head as if it is no big deal. I think everyone has seen him do it but no one has the heart to point it out.

I don't think Paul would shower once on this whole trip if Andrea and Tyson didn't force him to. I was glad they did. We all were. We ended up using the locker-room showers for the local college's indoor pool and got to swim for a while. I'd never been to an indoor pool before. There was a diving board and I tried my first backflip ever. All I can say is that it didn't go well. Instead of rotating, I went straight up in the air, and then smacked the water with the worst back-flop you could imagine. I don't think my back has ever been so red. Matt was on his school's diving team back home and was talking the rest of us into trying different flips and dives that we had no business attempting. And then he would laugh and say, "No, no. Not like that. Try it so it looks like this," and pull off some crazy dive.

He was a natural. It all seemed so effortless for him. It drove me crazy how easy he made it all look. He kept on coaching me, and by the time we were ready to leave I could do a front flip to a dive no problem. I doubted that I would ever try a backflip again though.

2:30 pm: It feels great to be clean again.

Our next stop was the grocery store. Shopping went much smoother this time around. My cook group decided to make hamburgers for dinner. I hadn't had a burger since being back home and I figured it was the longest time in my life I'd gone without one. Of course we had to get some veggie burgers too. When Allen found out I'd never tried one he made me promise that I would. We'll see.

8:30 pm: After we picked up our groceries we drove to a campground and set up camp. We had time to relax and take it easy all afternoon. And guess what, I tried a veggie burger for dinner. It wasn't even that bad either. I guess Allen is a pretty good guy after all. I told him he was my Hero-of-the-day and I thought he was going to cry he was so happy.

DAY TWENTY-ONE:

10:45 am: After a long breakfast we drove to some nature preserve to start our community service project. We were supposed to help rebuild a hiking bridge, but we had a change of plans at the last minute.

When we showed up, the only thing waiting for us was our guide and you could tell right away that he was drunk. It wasn't even lunchtime yet. He was some volunteer that was supposed to be managing us and the project we were working on. But there were no supplies, and no tools except for two shovels.

The boozer's cheeks were splotchy and red, as if his skin was tired of the body it had been dealt and decided to slowly start peeling away. It was disgusting. He tried to tell Tyson that we were supposed to dig four holes on each side of some creek a couple miles up the trail. Each hole was supposed to be four feet deep. Andrea looked at him like he was crazy. She asked him straight up, "With two shovels? You're joking right?"

Then he said something back to her. I couldn't hear what he said because I was too far away, but she sure didn't like whatever it was because her immediate response was, "Well thank you for your time, but unfortunately this is not going to work out. I will contact your organization and let them know. LET'S GO EVERYONE, BACK IN THE VAN!"

I had no idea Andrea had that kind of fight in her. She was always so patient with us, but that guy must have said something awfully disrespectful because she lit up like a firecracker. We drove back towards town and found a park to have lunch. The whole time Tyson wouldn't shut up about what a bad-ass Andrea was and how nobody better disrespect our group or we will introduce them to her. She was still pretty worked up and you could tell that she appreciated his attempt to make light of the situation.

96

The two of them spent the whole lunch talking in private trying to figure out what we were gonna do for the next few days now that our original plan was out the window. Finally they gathered us all around and Andrea started on about how there was no way we were going to spend the summer in Alaska without seeing a grizzly bear. Right away Tyson interrupted and corrected her, "We call them *brown bears* up here little lady."

It was pretty cool that he was able to make fun of himself about that, and we all got a kick out of it. I loved it when the two of them fed off of each other.

1:30 pm: Andrea ended up surprising us and driving to the Alaska Zoo so that we could go back home saying we got to see a grizzly in Alaska. Unfortunately we just found out the zoo is way more expensive than she thought it would be.

Since going to the zoo wasn't officially part of the trip, Andrea and Tyson couldn't use the company credit card for the tickets. But they weren't going to give up that easy. They ran off and no less than five minutes later told us they were able to get us all in the park for free. Andrea explained, "The only catch is that we agreed to do some maintenance in exchange for our entry into the park."

"Nothing's really free: great life lesson kids," Tyson sarcastically chimed in while she continued to explain.

"Besides, this will count kind of like our community service for today, and by tomorrow we will figure something else out."

Tyson added, "So once we clean out the Yak pen we will have the rest of the day to explore the zoo!"

In a sarcastic and unenthusiastic unison we gave them what they were waiting for, "YAY..."

Needless to say their excitement level was a bit higher than ours.

"Wait, what's that mean?" asked Jennifer.

"It means we've got to go pick up Yak crap, what do you think it means?" Jeff snapped back.

Believe it or not, it wasn't as bad as I expected. We ended up making the trashcans into targets to hurl the Yak poop at from across the pen. Everyone thought it was gross at first, but soon we all joined in. If danger could be turned into entertainment as quick as it had been with Tyson and the campfire the other night, a dirty job could be transformed even quicker.

After we finished with the poop, we all got to roam around the zoo for the afternoon. It was a pretty cool zoo as far as I could tell, although Allen kept complaining that there wasn't enough room for the animals to roam and that the place was really just a prison in disguise. Jeff and I gave him a hard time about it till we realized how much it really bothered him. We left him at the petting zoo where he could make a better connection with the inmates. It seemed to really cheer him up.

Then we made our way to the grizzly exhibit and ran into Tyson and Andrea. After seeing how big a grizzly was in real life, I hoped that the zoo was the only place I would ever have to see one. I leaned over and joked with Tyson, "Ain't nothing a little bear spray and a pocket knife couldn't handle, right Tyson?"

He chuckled to himself. All he could say was, "Right... right," as he stared with the amazement and wonder of a small child.

That night we relaxed back at the new campground we were staying at. Some people camping next to us had a guitar, and Tyson borrowed it to play for us. Everyone knew the words to almost all the songs he was playing except me. I never even heard of half of them, even though I could tell that they were all classic songs people would expect to hear sitting around a campfire. I felt embarrassed so I went for a walk and found a good place to smoke.

I watched the sun try to set, but it doesn't really work like that up here.

You see, there were these mountains way off in the distance. And the sun was just moving at the slightest downward angle toward the horizon. But mostly it was moving from left to right. For a while, it would disappear behind one of the peaks, only to reappear again on the other side. It was kind of like a series of several quick sunsets and sunrises all rolled into one viewing. And it was almost eleven o'clock at night. I still couldn't get over the lack of darkness.

DAY TWENTY-TWO:

9:15 am: We all got to sleep in and woke up to the smell of homemade pancakes. It was the first hot breakfast besides instant oatmeal we had all trip. And hands down the best pancakes I have ever had.

Tyson and Andrea woke up early to make them for us. But they weren't ordinary pancakes. See, Andrea was kind of a health-nut and Tyson was a straight up chocoholic. So half the pancakes were made with fruit and berries while the other half were chocolate. Not just chocolate-chip though. Tyson chopped up just about every different kind of chocolate candy bar there was and mixed them into the batter. It was almost too much.

10:30 am: After breakfast we decided we would make a bunch of burritos and hand them out to the ~~bums~~ homeless population of Anchorage for our community service project. We drove around first to see if we could find a central area where they hung out. It was kind of shocking that we were able to find so many homeless people up here. I wonder what they do in the wintertime.

Allen was the one who suggested the idea and everyone was much more excited about giving people food instead of digging holes in the ground for our project.

Andrea and Tyson explained that what we were doing didn't offer any sort of a long term solution for the homeless. How handing out food was more like a Band-Aid, because we were treating a symptom rather than the problem. But no matter what, a warm meal could mean the world sometimes. Even more importantly, Andrea stressed that the human connection—eye contact and a smile—was far more important than most could ever imagine.

12:45 pm: We went back to the grocery store and cooked up some beans and rice on our camp stove in the parking lot. All in all we made just under a hundred burritos. Before heading out to the streets, we each ate one for lunch.

When Josh realized a burrito would be the only thing we were going to eat he raised his concern, "I don't want one. I thought we were making these for the homeless, not us."

I could tell that he was disgusted by them. Tyson chuckled and replied, "It is a fool who thinks he is better than the food he makes for others."

Josh just looked confused.

"We should feel lucky for what we have Josh," Tyson went on, "It is important to keep as much of a connection as possible to those you are trying to help. Besides, it can be dangerous while developing your character to come to a conclusion about most things until you have experienced them for yourself."

As it turned out, the burritos tasted pretty damn good, and I could tell Josh felt foolish for making a scene. I held off the urge to rub it in his face and tried to make him feel better by telling him not to worry about it too much.

3:15 pm: We split up into groups of three when it was time to hand out our burritos and I ended up with Paul and Lucy. We all stayed within eye contact of Tyson and Andrea the whole time, which was part of their rules.

At first we were nervous walking around, not sure if we should be scared by what we saw. I wasn't even sure who was homeless and who wasn't sometimes, and really didn't want to offend anyone. The whole thing was kind of depressing, seeing people live like that. But it felt very rewarding when someone would say thanks, and I knew they really meant it. Some people wouldn't accept our burritos, just too suspicious I guess. Poor Paul, no one seemed to want a burrito from him at all. It must have been his delivery because I wasn't having any problems. Most of the people were very nice and it gave me a special feeling knowing that we were helping others with no strings attached.

Most of the bums, I mean homeless people, in Anchorage were flat out drunks, you could smell it on them. I kept thinking about the conversation I had with Katie and Steve when we were sea kayaking. About how that characteristic, the fact they were mostly drunks, was really just the tip of the iceberg as far as who these people were. I wondered how they ended up on the streets, and where they came from. Most of all, I thought about what was going to happen to them, if they would ever be able to get things together again.

Some of them clearly had mental issues, and that made me the saddest because I could tell they were suffering, and needed real help. I remembered my grandpa talking about bums one Christmas when I was a kid and how they just needed to quit being lazy and get over whatever put them on the streets in the first place. Maybe that was where I got my thoughts on the subject from. I wondered if he ever met a homeless person before, ever talked to one. Because if he had, I doubt he would still be saying the same old thing. And I understood what Tyson meant about those who come to rushed conclusions about things they know very little about. All my grandpa had ever known about homeless people was the tip to a massive iceberg hidden beneath the surface. He wasn't wrong necessarily. But there was much more to it, that's all.

We had almost gotten rid of all our burritos when a cop drove by. He stopped and put on his lights, then called us over to him. He didn't know what to make of us at first. After Tyson told him what we were doing the cop told us that we were all going to receive a citation for the distribution of food without a license. I couldn't believe it! Then Jeff spat out, "Why do you gotta be such a dick, man? We are just trying to help other people."

The cop didn't even look up as he said, "Just following orders son."

Tyson told us to shut up and I could tell he meant it. Then he asked the cop if they could discuss the matter in private. Andrea stayed with us and tried to defend the cop for just following his orders, although I don't think she was fooling anyone. It was obvious she was upset about the whole thing just as much as anyone else.

Jeff started on a rant, "Just following orders? That's the most pathetic thing I've ever hear. That was the Nazi's excuse for killing the Jews too. Just following orders! That guy needs to learn how to think for himself and distinguish the difference between criminals and humanitarians. Just following orders? Ever hear about the banality of evil? It's how pigs like that are able to feel good about ticketing kids who are trying to help others. Just following orders! People need to learn how to think for themselves. This is exactly why I question authority, you know? Because authority always manages to miraculously lose the ability to question itself."

He was over all of our heads and I told Jeff to give it a rest. That he wasn't helping the situation. His response was short, "Well just because it isn't helping *this* situation doesn't make it any less important."

Maybe he had a point, but there had to be a better way to make it. In the end Tyson was able to talk the cop into only issuing one ticket, which Tyson accepted graciously. We still had a couple dozen burritos left and were happy to eat them ourselves rather than throw them out in front of the cop. Tyson kept trying to get the cop to eat one, and for a second, I thought the cop was going to. I couldn't believe how cool Tyson and Andrea stayed throughout the whole thing. By the time we left, you could tell the cop felt pretty bad about giving Tyson a ticket.

5 pm: After we finished up with the burritos we had the rest of the afternoon to explore. The leaders gave us some time to walk around the touristy part of Anchorage so long as we promised to stay in groups of three or more. All the boys went together and same with the girls.

We wandered around aimlessly for a while until we came across a knife shop. Every one of the boys bought a knife. Except for me that is. I wanted to, you see, but I decided not to after all. Not just cause I didn't have very much money, or the fact that it would have been against my probation. But the real reason was I knew that a weapon wasn't the sort of thing I needed. Not till I could control myself better anyways.

It's funny because I always wanted a knife back home, you know, for security. Protection. But if you pull out a knife, you better be ready to use it. I guess I don't really want a knife because I know that I *am* capable of using it. And maybe people like me, ones that are capable of using something like that, don't need to own stuff like that in the first place.

I mean honestly, when am I ever going to really need a knife? Sure there were a million reasons I could list off, but I couldn't help think of what Tyson said about perceived risks versus real risks, and how most of the reasons I could mention were most likely never going to happen anyways. It felt good to be able to control the impulse. It felt good to be able to see things from a larger perspective.

10 pm: I ended up speaking more at tonight's meeting then I ever had before. I talked about making the choice to not buy a knife today and how I focused on the real applications of it versus the perceived ones. Tyson seemed impressed and challenged all of us to question the decisions we make in our lives. He encouraged us to question everything we're taught before accepting anything as absolute. He said that he didn't care if people thought the same things he did, he just wanted people to think. To think for themselves.

That night when Tyson was away for a minute we all decided to pitch in and pay the seventy bucks for the ticket the cop issued him. "Solidarity" is what Allen called it, and I found myself desperate to believe in what he was pushing. I wasn't that different from Allen after all. We all want to believe in something. He just wasn't ever afraid to give it a try.

It felt good to know that I was surrounded by such thoughtful people. People I had written off because they were rich, because they were different. But the more time we spent together, the more I was beginning to focus on our similarities rather than our differences. Everyone agreed that a real transformation was underway. I told them it wouldn't have been possible without their support and that I was just grateful for a true second chance from them. I was.

DAY TWENTY-THREE:

11 am: Woke up and prepared for another long drive day. I chose to sit in the middle row next to Steve and Sarah. We've been talking about all sorts of stuff, but mostly what we want to do with our lives.

Personally, I had no idea what I wanted to do. Of course I thought about it before, but it usually overwhelms me till I feel paralyzed. Like a deer in headlights or something. But the way Steve was talking about his future got me thinking. He wants to become a professional photographer. He was so passionate about it. He said it was because taking pictures allowed him to express himself creatively. That he felt like an artist every time he looked through the lens.

I tried to think about how I expressed myself creatively. I had never even really thought about it before. There were plenty of things I liked to do, but none of them were really outlets for my creativity.

Steve showed me some of the basics as far as how his fancy camera worked. I was taking pictures of everyone in the van and got a couple of pretty good shots. Steve was impressed anyways. He told me I could take as many pictures as I wanted and that he would send them to me, which was good because I didn't even bring a camera on the trip. Didn't think I would need one. Didn't think I would want one.

As for Sarah, she didn't really know what she wanted to do just like me. But there was plenty of stuff she didn't want to do with her life. For one thing, she didn't want to stay in Vegas. Both Sarah and her sister Katie were always talking about moving away as soon as they were old enough. She didn't know where she wanted to live, "maybe somewhere with lots of nature," she said as she stared off at the scenery passing us by at sixty miles an hour. She told us that she wanted to do something with animals, maybe horses. That she always had a better connection with animals than with people.

I never have been into animals much myself. My dad had a dog when I was little, but it was too aggressive with me so it always stayed outside and I always stayed inside. Even though I couldn't relate to what Sarah was saying, I enjoyed listening to her go on and on about it. She was a real free spirit and her energy was contagious.

Sarah was the same age as me, and our birthdays were only a couple of weeks apart. She was religious, but not nearly as much as I would think she would be for growing up home schooled in the back of a church. She was funny too. I mean real funny. She had all these witty comebacks to everything, and was always laughing at herself, so you couldn't help but laugh with her. She was prettier than her sister Katie, with a short bob cut. And she wore these red rimmed glasses. I have always had a thing for glasses on a girl. I don't know why, I just have.

Steve eventually nodded off and Sarah and I talked for hours. It was the most I had ever talked to a girl before. Usually I'd run out of stuff to say pretty quick, but not with Sarah. She had this way of making me feel comfortable, like I could say anything.

2:30 pm: I know most of the group can't stand these long drive days but I don't mind them at all. They are relaxing. And we got to stop for ice cream after our lunch.

I even had a conversation with Lyle today. First one since our fight. It wasn't much, but it was something. He mostly told me about Manhattan and what a cool place it was to live. I guess it would be if you had a lot of money, but I didn't mention that to him. At first it was hard not to throw in a jab when he would set himself up, but after a while I was less focused on how to make fun of him and mostly just curious about New York City.

7:50 pm: I was asleep when we pulled into the campground. Our river guides were already there waiting for us. They got dropped off with all of the boats and gear we were going to need. They came over to introduce themselves but that was it. They told us they would see us in the morning and explain everything then.

Their campsite was far away from ours, but we could hear them all night. It sounded like a party. Tyson and Andrea went to go talk to them and were gone for hours. Who knows what they were doing.

As for us, Tyson left Lucy in charge of the fire. I guess he figured she wouldn't let it get out of control and the rest of us would listen to her. We stayed up late talking and laughing, roasting marshmallows. And I was truly enjoying myself with the group. Hell, I felt like I was part of it.

DAY TWENTY-FOUR:

9:45 am: Woke up early and packed up camp, then met up with our river guides. Each of us was issued a lifejacket, helmet, and dry-suit. A dry-suit is this outfit you have to wear to keep from getting wet. The water we are going to be rafting in is straight from some glacier, and is ~~cold as hell~~ freezing. The guides told us you could die from how cold it was without one of these suits. You have to wear sweats under the dry-suit and the only things exposed are your hands and your head. Lucky for us, we got gloves too.

Then we went over some basic training on how to paddle and what to do if one of the rafts flips upside down. We loaded all the gear onto the boats and are about to take off downriver. We are going to be gone for six days, so there is a ton of gear. There are four boats total. Two for us and two for all the gear we need.

Within the first ten minutes Paul managed to fall overboard. There weren't any rapids or anything, he just fell backwards for no particular reason at all. The guides couldn't stop laughing at Paul just floating on his back like he was in a backyard pool or something and told us we could all jump in if we wanted to. Anyone who didn't jump in right away got pushed in by Tyson. I made sure to jump before he got to me. It felt so strange swimming and feeling totally dry at the same time. Except for my head of course. The water was so cold it gave me a headache as soon as my head went under.

4:30 pm: The rest of the first day on the river was pretty mellow without very many rapids. We made camp early, right there on the side of the river, and I have to admit that the scenery was striking. Tyson found some wood and showed us the technique for busting, but no one was able to start a fire. It seemed like it wasn't necessarily a difficult thing to do, you just needed to be smooth and patient. Here is a picture.

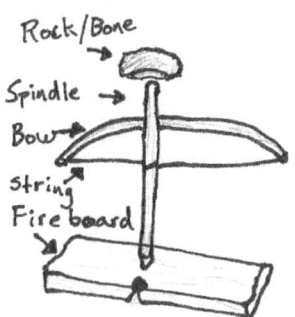

It seemed easy until I tried. It is mainly just a back and forth motion with a stick shaped like a bow with a thin rope or string attached to both ends. You have to wrap another stick, called a spindle, one time around the rope. Then you have to place the bottom end of the spindle into a V-shaped notch carved out of the fireboard, which is a flat piece of wood that rests on the ground. Next you apply pressure to the top of the spindle with something to protect the palm of your hand that still allows the spindle to spin back and forth. A smooth concave rock or another piece of wood could do the trick, but Tyson found an old knee bone from a deer for us to use. The spindle fit perfect inside of it and you could get a back and forth motion going much easier.

The other thing that is really important when trying to make a fire using friction is the type of wood. Tyson told us that cottonwood trees worked best, but since there weren't any of those around he used pieces of aspen for the fireboard and willow for the spindle and bow, but anything works for the bow so long as it bends.

There's a lot more to it of course, but the main thing I couldn't believe was how much energy it took to move the bow back and forth while applying enough friction between the spindle and the fireboard. My spindle kept falling out of the notch in the fireboard and I became exhausted before I could ever get an ember going. It was a humbling experience for all of us.

The sun came out for a little bit and Sarah used her glasses to ignite a flame. She just laughed at all of us and reminded us to work smarter rather than harder. None of us seemed to find it as amusing as she did.

9 pm: Tonight's dinner was amazing. Hot dogs and beans cooked on the campfire. I felt like I was a cowboy from the Wild West. Everyone kept farting during the meeting because of it. Even Tyson gave up on trying to keep things serious and was letting them rip too. It was hilarious.

It was clear by now that the group was serious about giving me a second chance. I knew how lucky I was, and was trying to give everyone a chance myself, something I never used to do. Mostly I just tried getting to know everyone better. Even Lyle, kind of. And the more I did, the more fun I started to have. I know people always tell you junk like that, but it's true, I swear. You get what you give. I was still trying to kick some old habits of course, but I could tell that things were improving. Everyone could.

DAY TWENTY-FIVE:

12:30 pm: We started seeing some bigger rapids today. They are fun, but they can be scary too. One of the boats flipped in a rapid early on and everyone had to swim to shore. The guides were all laughing and said that paddle boats flipped there all the time, but it was no big deal because the rapid wasn't too dangerous and there was a long calm downstream. The gear boats knew better and paddled around that rapid.

We stopped for lunch right before the biggest rapid of the trip. The guides call it "Granny's Washing Machine." We all hiked downstream and watched the water fight against gravity, using the massive boulders standing strong and spread throughout the river to delay the inevitable push towards the salty ocean. I'm feeling nervous, but excited too.

The guide in our boat was named Anna. She pointed out all of the hazards and where to swim and where not to swim if we fell out. But she stressed over and over again the importance of not falling out of the boat in this particular rapid. Tyson told her that he would sit next to Paul and personally ensure he remained in the raft. We all laughed, but I was kind of nervous for Paul. He had already fallen out four times.

After lunch settled, we shoved off and prepared ourselves for what looked to be impossible. As we approached, we couldn't actually see any of the rapids at first. Instead it looked calm for a few hundred feet and then the waterline just kind of disappeared. But we could hear it all right. It sounded like thunder and I started feeling my nerves kick in. Anna could tell too. "NERVOUS?!" she yelled. The river guides always yelled everything when we were in the boat.

I told her I wasn't and she just laughed. "Well I am," she said, "only reason I do this job. For the nerves! Reminds me I'm still alive. YEE-HAW!" And whether she had intended it or not, I suddenly got a whole lot more nervous.

The plan was to start on the far right side of the river. Once we passed the first small rapid, we would have to paddle as fast as we could to get to the far left side of the river for the rest of the rapids to avoid a small waterfall. Matt asked why we couldn't just go through that part and our guide Anna explained that there was something called a hole below the drop that could keep holding a person under the water for several minutes at a time till they drowned, and that was why we were avoiding it. Hearing all that didn't help my nerves one bit. And then the unthinkable happened.

Right at the top of the first rapid, the one on the right side, Sarah fell out of the boat. It all happened in a split second, but it seemed like an eternity. She looked so helpless and scared. Without thinking twice, I jumped in after her. Everyone was freaking out and the guides were all yelling. The guide in our boat was yelling at everyone else to keep paddling, so that they didn't gut the nasty part of the lower rapid, while the guide in the boat behind us stood up screaming and pointing for Sarah and me to try to swim to the left too. But all I could think about was getting to Sarah.

I reached her right before we went over the falls of the big rapid. We didn't even make it close to swimming to the left. She was too frozen with fear and I was swimming as hard as I could to catch up to her. I was able to grab her wrist right as we were going over the falls. I was only able to hold on for a split second, but in that time I tried to look in her eyes and let her know that everything was going to be fine, even if it wasn't.

As soon as we went over the falls, I lost her, and for a second I thought that I had lost her for good. The rapids did their best to drown me, and I found myself stuck in the hole that our guide Anna warned us about.

The water was so cold, and I could feel it leaking in from the neck of my dry-suit. When I realized that I wasn't floating up to the surface I opened my eyes. There were so many air bubbles in the water that I couldn't see a thing, except that sunlight was coming from where I thought the ground was. I was upside down and didn't even know it. Then right-side up, then back upside down again. I began to feel like I was in a washing machine. Time stood still. I struggled to make it to the surface but there was no use. Then, all of a sudden I bumped into something. Sarah! It had to be. And just like that she was gone again. My imminent death was even worse knowing I failed to save her.

A few seconds later, my feet were pushed against the ground. I pushed back with everything I had, and in the process got spit out fifty feet downstream where the water started to grow calm again.

Everyone was yelling different things to me, but all I could think about was Sarah. Then I saw her on the shore, with one of the guides. The other boats made it through fine, and eddied out downstream. That's what you call it when a boat goes to the side of the river where the current isn't very strong.

Sarah was pretty shook up by the whole experience. I wanted to talk to her but the guides told me to give her a minute. They were all very upset with me for jumping out after her, and told me how lucky I was to be alive. I asked how long I was in the hole for and they said close to thirty seconds. I could have sworn it had been an hour. When I explained what happened in the hole, how I bumped into Sarah, our guide Anna patted me on the back. Then she said, "As crazy as that was, she could have been stuck in there a long time if you hadn't bumped her out like that. Probably saved her life, you know."

"But I couldn't hold on to her. I let her go." And I felt terrible for that.

Anna tried to console me, telling me no one could have held on through a rapid like that. That I did the best I could. And that was all anyone could hope for.

"But what happens when your best just isn't good enough?" and the way that I asked she could tell that I needed an honest answer.

"Well kid, we do what we can and we have to accept that sometimes things are just out of our reach."

Then Anna went on to tell me a story about a helicopter crash she was in a few years back. You see, in the winter time Anna was a heli-ski guide. That's where people go skiing and snowboarding using a helicopter to get to the top of a mountain. I could tell she was bad-ass already, but this took her to the next level for sure.

"So we were out in the middle of nowhere and had an engine malfunction. I knew what it meant before any of the guests did, so I told them to buckle up quick and hold on tight. I tightened down my seat-belt and braced for impact. I remember watching the ground turn sideways real slow, and then upside down all of a sudden. The pilot, well he died on impact. Nothing anyone could do about him. But everyone else was alive and I did the best I could to keep it that way. But like I said, sometimes some things are just out of our reach."

She was so calm as she was explaining it all, and it made my ordeal with the rapid seem like a walk in the park. She continued after a moment of silence, "Unfortunately I couldn't control the bleeding of one of the guests and he ended up dying right there in my arms. For a long time I thought that there was something that I could have done differently, to keep him alive. But like *you* said, sometimes our best just isn't good enough. The important thing is that we never stop trying."

After a minute or so I had to ask her something, "So wait a minute. Are you still a heli-ski guide?"

"Hell yeah, best job in the world."

"But even after the helicopter crash? Even after, you know?"

"Like *I* said kid, sometimes we have to accept that things are just out of our reach. But it doesn't do any good to dwell on things we have no control over. Shit happens all the time. It's not the *shit* that counts, it's how we deal with it. You know what I mean?"

Then she stood up and hollered to the group that it was time to move on and get to our campsite a few miles downriver. She was the burliest person I had ever met.

Sarah was still on edge, fortunately there weren't any more big rapids the rest of the afternoon. She insisted on sitting next to me in the boat and told me how much it meant to her when she was in the water. How she thought she was going to die of a heart attack until she saw me jump in after her. How it helped her when she knew that she wasn't going to go through the ringer on her own. I told her it was no big deal, and that I'd do it again if I needed to. She smiled and must've thanked me a hundred more times.

That evening I was her hero during the meeting. In fact, I was everyone's hero, although I still didn't feel like one. I told Sarah that she was mine for making it through "Granny's Washing Machine" in one piece. I had a second hero too. Our river guide Anna for sharing such a hard truth in such an honest way. Her approach to life was unparalleled by anyone else I had ever met. It was too ballsy for my blood, but I had to respect someone who lived out their passions on a day to day basis like she did.

After the meeting we listened to the guides tell more stories by the fire. Sarah wouldn't leave my side the whole time. When she was ready for bed she asked me to walk her to her tent. I did and before we got there she started kissing me. The whole thing caught me off guard. It was perfect really. The moon lit the ripples on the river while the sun took a siesta behind one of the far off peaks. We kissed for a long time. I put my hand under her shirt till she stopped me. She smiled, we kissed some more, and then I left for my tent, though I couldn't sleep. I was up all night trying to process everything that had happened.

DAY TWENTY-SIX:

9:45 am: We got to sleep in this morning while the guides cooked breakfast for us. Bacon and eggs! During breakfast Anna kept asking Tyson questions. She'd heard about him from past trip leaders. But there was one story she kept asking about. Something to do with him chugging a gallon of milk.

"So is it true you can't turn down a challenge Tyson?" she asked him playfully.

"Of course I can, and would," he chuckled, "It is just that there has never happened to be a challenge I needed to turn down."

"I heard you could chug a gallon of milk."

"And?"

"Well, I also heard that it's impossible."

He clarified, "It is impossible to drink a gallon of milk in less than an hour without throwing up."

"So?"

"So what?"

"So how long did it take you then?"

"To chug a gallon of milk? About three minutes."

"So you did the impossible then?"

"No." He answered casually. But then he looked around with a bashful grin before deciding to go on. "I was challenged by this other leader, a six-nippled man from Montana named Nathan, to see who could drink a gallon of milk faster."

"Wait! What?" It was at this point that everyone perked up and gathered around for the details.

"I was challenged to see who could…"

"No. Not that part. How many nipples did he have?"

"Who?"

"Dammit Tyson, you know who. The guy from Montana. How many?"

"Six."

"I don't believe you."

"Most people don't, and I don't expect you to either, but I'm telling you that I saw it with my own eyes. They ran right on down his belly, I swear. Each pair was smaller than the previous, but I assure you the man had six nipples. Andrea saw them too, ask her."

"Tyson is telling the truth," Andrea confirmed, "Although I saw it and I still don't believe it."

Anna was trying to visualize it as Tyson pointed out where they were on his chest. We all were. Anna finally regained focus and pressed on, "Wait, I still don't understand. What am I missing here?"

"Well, our challenge had nothing to do with throwing up. It was the last day of our company's training, and there was some extra food that we were trying to get rid of before it went bad. We were camping and there were no neighbors to offer stuff up to. So Nathan, the man with six nipples approached me with two one-gallon jugs of milk…"

"Whole milk or skim?"

"One percent, I think. Anyways, he bet that he could finish one before me, and that was how it all began."

"But I still don't understand."

"Well about half way through we were dead even, but I could feel something bad was about to happen. All of a sudden I just puked. Milk sprayed everywhere like when a fire hydrant opens up. As soon as I did, Nathan followed suit. But I had a challenge to win, so I went right back to chugging down my gallon of milk."

Everyone was gagging and telling Tyson how gross he was. He loved it.

"It *was* gross, and everyone was watching, including my boss. People were taking pictures; the whole thing was a mess, but I finished the challenge."

He sat there reflecting with a smile on his face. Then he added, "Couldn't eat ice cream for a year after that, and I love ice cream. Heck, I think I am lactose-intolerant now because of that little challenge."

"But you eat cheese all the time! I saw you add a ton of it to your eggs just now."

"I know, it just means that I fart a lot more now," and just then he ripped one of the longest farts I ever heard. Jennifer and Katie were grossed out, but everyone else was dying from laughter.

"Wait," Andrea added, "You are leaving out the best part."

"What's that?" Tyson asked.

"You know, about the fifty-fifty bar."

Tyson chuckled to himself. Then he added, "Oh yeah. Well, before Nathan found me someone else came around with a gallon of orange juice. I must have drank half of that jug too."

"So?" Jeff asked.

"So, every time that I threw up, it tasted like a fifty-fifty bar on the way out. Which made the whole thing way more enjoyable.

Heck, I probably wouldn't have been able to finish if my puke didn't taste so good coming back up."

Everyone was grossed out while simultaneously dying from laughter. It took us all morning to even get started rafting.

4:45 pm: Tyson's goofiness set the tone for the rest of the day. We goofed around during the flat parts of the river, but always got focused when a rapid section came up. Probably because of what happened to Sarah yesterday. We all knew how serious the river could be. And if you weren't serious about it, you could get yourself into a lot of trouble.

One of the other river guides said it best, "If you piss on the river, the river will piss on you."

At our meeting that night Sarah told us that she felt much more comfortable on the river than she did the day before. Tyson's response was deep as usual, "I'm glad to hear it Sarah, time has that effect."

Sarah thought about it and then replied, "Part of it is that. But I think what really helped was how we could all switch from goofing around to being serious when we needed to. I felt like we were all on the same page. And that I could trust that no one was going to screw things up for the rest of us."

I felt like crap. She didn't mean it, but that was exactly what I had done the first part of the trip.

Allen added, "I guess it's kind of an easy lesson to learn on a river. You know, cause it's easy to tell when the switch is coming. You know, between the time for fun and the time to be serious."

"If only life was as easy to read as a river." I mumbled to myself. I wished that it was.

DAY TWENTY-SEVEN:

1:30 pm: All I can say is that I love rafting. I get it. The river that is. And the rapids. They scare the crap out of me but they are so much fun. Especially now that we know how to navigate the boats so well. We are like a fine-tuned machine. We can navigate through anything and our guides have noticed. All morning long we nailed rapid after rapid, and no one fell out once. Not even Paul.

All during lunch the entire group laughed and had a great time complementing each other on how well we were working together. We were a team, and it felt good to be a part of it.

6 pm: The afternoon went even better than the morning. So much fun! The guides won't stop talking about how good we did. Everyone still has so much energy I think it is going to be a good meeting this evening.

After we all shared our highlights and heroes, Josh, he was the Leader-of-the-day, asked a really tough question. He was the one kid I still didn't know very well besides Lyle. Nobody knew him that well really. Just that he always bragged about how much crap his dad bought him and that he felt like a zombie from his meds. He really did seem like a zombie most of the time. And so nobody tried to get to know him because he never tried either.

So out of nowhere he asked us without it seeming like he put much thought into it, "Okay you guys, what is the worst thing that has ever happened to you?"

Just the way he asked, I could tell that the worst thing that ever happened to him was that his parents probably bought him a green car when he wanted a red one, or something lame like that.

At first Andrea and Tyson weren't sure if it was an appropriate question, but pretty much everyone agreed that they were alright with it. Most of the answers were pretty run of the mill. Stuff you would expect. A fight with parents, losing a pet, stuff like that. Until it was Lucy's turn. She wasn't her usual bubbly and sweet self. Instead she seemed quiet and withdrawn. I remembered she was one of the ones that didn't say she was fine with answering the question. Then again, she didn't speak up against it either. All she said for her answer was that she lost someone very close to her.

No tears, no emotion at all really.

No one knew what to do. Fortunately Andrea was sitting next to her. She casually put her hand over Lucy's shoulder and began to answer the question herself. You could tell that Josh was beginning to understand the consequences of such a poorly thought out question, but it was too late to take it back.

When it was Katie's turn she stayed quiet for a long time. Josh made it worse by reminding her that it was her turn. She told him that she was well aware of this fact.

When she was good and ready she told us how a member of her church had touched her inappropriately when she was younger. But that the worst part was that no one believed her when she said something, because the man had such a good reputation and she was known as a girl who was hungry for attention. Her own parents didn't even believe her and asked her to stop pushing the issue, so she did. They told her to pray about the pain she had caused the man by spreading such a rumor. As if it couldn't get much worse, she still saw him every week in church. Nothing ever happened again, but seeing him every week was very difficult for her. The only reason she still went was to make sure that nothing ever happened to her sister.

A few of the girls started crying. But Lucy, she was really beginning to lose it. Tyson and Andrea had no idea what to do; you couldn't just turn off all of those emotions. And even if you could, maybe it would be worse to just pretend like nothing ever happened.

Lucy wasn't trying to steal the attention from Katie, but people began to ask her to say what was wrong. When Katie asked her to share, Lucy reluctantly agreed.

Lucy was molested too. But hers was a very different experience. And it all came out, whether she wanted it to or not. When Lucy was thirteen she and her best friend used to tell each other's parents that they were each spending the night at the other girl's house, and then go hang out around town all night. They never really did much, just walked around mostly, tried to smoke cigarettes Lucy would steal from her older brother, looked for boys to flirt with, the usual stuff.

One night Lucy wanted to walk around the streets at two in the morning. Her friend was tired, but Lucy talked her into it anyways. They were going to go watch the drunks leave the local bar when a van rolled up on them. All Lucy remembered was being hit from the side. When she woke up she was in a hospital. She had been raped by numerous men and parts of her body had been seriously mutilated. Her friend was even worse off, and ended up dying in the hospital.

As if Lucy hadn't been through enough, her friend's mother held Lucy responsible for her daughter's death, and made a terrible scene at the hospital. So much so that Lucy began to feel guilty for what happened to her and her friend.

Lucy's family ended up moving out of state to get a new start. She began intensive therapy. The men were never found.

Lucy was calmly rocking herself back and forth, and you could tell she was reliving horrific memories that had no need to be brought up on a night like this one. No one knew if it was better to try to hold her or if touching her might make things worse. So we all did the worst thing we could in a situation like that: nothing.

Finally Katie spoke up, "So that was the person who you lost that was close to you. I am so, so very sorry."

Lucy sniffled and an uncomfortable smile overcame her. "No," she said.

Back home Lucy had an older brother and sister. When they moved to Colorado the family tried their best to get on with their lives, but that was pretty much impossible. Her parents devoted their lives to helping Lucy move past her experience, and in the process the other two siblings seemed to fall by the wayside. Her brother was already dealing with depression, and the move—along with everything else—didn't help. He took his own life a year and a half later. Lucy interpreted the note he left behind to confirm her deepest fears, that his death was somehow her fault too.

I thought about the note I had written my parents as she explained all this, and how it never even crossed my mind how they would have probably held themselves responsible too, even though it wasn't their fault either.

No matter what anyone said, Lucy felt like she was now responsible for two other people's tragic endings. She summed it all up so easily, "It wasn't my experience that was the worst thing that has ever happened to me. It is how it has affected the people I cared about the most."

Lucy had come on this trip to get away from her past. Her family still hadn't moved out of the house where her brother died and being there was too much during the summer when she didn't have school to keep her busy. Everyone felt her pain, but there was nothing we could do or say.

One by one we all wandered aimlessly off to bed; though I don't think anyone got much sleep.

DAY TWENTY-EIGHT:

11 am: Another day of rafting on the river. Not much more to say. Sorry. Everyone is just kind of in a funk.

I didn't know how to act around Lucy all morning. I still couldn't believe it. She was so sweet, so positive all the time. I would have never guessed in a million years that she had been through so much. I wished there was something I could do, but I didn't know what. It didn't seem like there was anything I could do to make it better. I wanted to hug her, hold her. Maybe tell her that everything was going to be alright. But that seemed like it would come off as some sort of sick joke, after what she had been through.

She could tell everyone felt uncomfortable about how to act. I felt like she hated that she shared such intimate details of her life. She kept catching me, just staring at her, which was only making it worse. During lunch she pulled me aside and called me out.

"What?" she demanded.

I stood there, full of emotion with no clue how to express it. My face was blank, and she probably had no idea what was going on in my brain. I couldn't even process it all.

"What?" she said again, "Don't make me wish I didn't tell you that."

"No. No, it's not that. I just…"

"What?"

"I just… I just wish…"

"That there was something you could do for me?"

125

And there was a moment that I hoped everything was going to be alright. That there *was* a way I could help. Something I could do or say that would solve her problems and make everything better.

"You really wish there was something you could do?"

I told her I did.

"Something to make it better?" she was stern and dead serious. Still genuine, but like I had never seen her before.

"Anything," I said, "And I will do it." I found myself caring more about helping this girl than anyone else in the entire world. A girl that I had written off as a spoiled rich kid just a couple of weeks ago. I hated myself for that now.

"Alright, fine. There is something."

I waited while she worked out in her head how to phrase it.

"Stop making rape jokes."

And right then and there my heart sunk.

"I've heard you," she went on, "You and Jeff. Making jokes about rape here and there. Like it's no big deal. The funniest thing in the world." And as she said it the softest tears you could imagine began to make a long and unnecessary journey from her deep brown eyes to the edge of her lifejacket pressing up against her pale neck.

"It's just that... I didn't know." I knew the last thing she wanted to hear was an excuse. It was the last thing I wanted to offer up, but it came out anyways.

But it didn't bother her. She looked at me, so genuine, so understanding. "I know," she said, "But that is the whole point. I bet you didn't know about Katie either. I bet there are a lot of girls that you don't know about that hear your little comments. Your jokes."

And as she kept talking her tears were now being mirrored by my own.

"And I know that you don't really mean anything by them," she continued, "At least I like to hope that you don't. You probably don't even realize when you are doing it sometimes. But you have no idea how much pain they can bring to someone who has been through anything like what I have. The memories that can resurface. And it only makes things worse when the pains from my past are written off as *baggage* by boys that don't even have a clue."

I was bawling now, because I knew that my ignorance had been anything but bliss to her and who knew how many other girls. But Lucy remained calm, her slow and steady stream of soft tears remaining the same as when it first began.

She went on, "You really have no idea how much fear you can bring to a girl, regardless of what has happened to her, with the reality of how casual you are able to be about such a serious thing."

Then she was quiet for a long time. She waited for my tears to match hers again. And in the end it was her that was hugging me. At that moment I understood just how strong she truly was.

I understood that there was no need to feel sorry for her. She didn't want that anyways. What she wanted from me really wouldn't take much effort at all.

All she wanted was for people like me to stop hurting others by trivializing something that we knew very little about. And I knew I could do that for her. I promised her I would.

9 pm: Everyone was beginning to come around by the evening's meeting. Tyson and Andrea were trying their best to keep things light without trying to pretend that last night never happened. When it was time for the

nightly question we all cringed at what might come out of Paul's mouth. His question for us was, "What's the hottest thing you have ever eaten?" It was the perfect question that made us all laugh and share stupid stories. My answer was a habanero pepper from my uncle's garden, and how he switched his out with something less spicy, so that I couldn't understand why my mouth was on fire and he was perfectly fine. I joked that I could have drank a gallon of milk in under two minutes without a problem that day just to cool down my mouth because the pepper was so hot. But Paul's answer was the craziest. He tried to eat a piece of dry ice once, and had to go to the hospital because of it.

By the end of the night it looked like we, as a group, were going to be just fine. I smiled at Lucy when she glanced over at me. She smiled back. Before going to sleep I thanked Paul for how well timed his question was, but who knows if he had any idea why I was thanking him.

DAY TWENTY-NINE:

6:15 am: Today is our last day on the river. There is something about floating down a river on a boat without a motor. It changes the way you look at things. Not just the scenery, but your perspective too. It can be the scariest thing ever one minute and then the calmest, most relaxing and peaceful time of your life the next. The current helps you along the way, but in the end, it is up to you to successfully navigate your way to where you want to go. Sometimes things go wrong, but you always seem to manage, and the mistakes become experiences that shape your memories and who you are for as long as you choose. Until you decide to forget them.

I wrote that in my journal early this morning before anyone else got up. I am more proud of it than anything else I have ever written. All it took was a little time and some effort.

I used to see my journal as a chore. A waste of time. Something that was for someone else's help, not mine. But as each day passed I realized that it was only what I made of it. Just writing the basics hadn't been doing all that much for me. But perhaps writing could become my creative outlet. I always hated writing in school. Reading too. I'd never really put that much into them, or school in general for that matter. The teachers could tell too. I always hated it when they called on me to answer a question they knew perfectly well that I didn't know the answer to. What were they trying to prove anyways? They should have just given up and stopped asking me questions all the time. I sure as hell wasn't going to start learning anything just so I could answer their dumb questions.

But maybe it wasn't really like that. Or didn't have to be at least. Don't get me wrong, I don't ever plan on being a straight A student or anything like that. But this trip, this journal, kept reminding me that I only get out what I put in. I had a choice to take something away from all of this. I wasted so much time by not applying myself earlier on. If only school were less boring. Maybe if it were taught on a river.

12:30: After lunch there are still lots of rapids, and one more big rapid section towards the end of the day. I know Sarah is scared. She made me promise that I would sit next to her through the rapid. I like that somebody looks to me for strength and support. That has never happened before. I hope that I don't let her down.

I tried to comfort her by talking about the difference between perceived risks and real risks, but the more I thought about it I was less sure which one river rafting fell under. All I knew was that I loved that feeling during the rapids, the rush. I think it has something to do with knowing that something could go terribly wrong at any moment, and no matter how well prepared I am there is nothing I can do to stop it.

I imagine a lot of people would get anxiety from the whole thing. Don't get me wrong, that feeling scares the crap out of me too. But still, there is something about the risk factor directly relating to the level of excitement. Maybe Tyson was missing something. Maybe sometimes you have to be willing to take big risks if you want big rewards. Great, I am starting to sound like one of those adrenaline junkies or something. Which I am not. Or never was before anyways.

Maybe there's a way to find a balance. When I asked Tyson about it he chuckled and kept things as vague as possible, "There is a time and a place for everything."

I told him I wasn't very impressed and he gave it another shot. He explained how within the realm of real risks there is a spectrum. How it was important to be able to distinguish between taking calculated risks like rafting with professional guides and safety gear, and uninformed risks like trying to kayak these rapids on your own if you had never been kayaking before and didn't know anything about rivers. He went on and on about learning curves and how as your ability improves, so does your chance of success. The whole thing was beginning to sound like a school lesson, which made me laugh, because I had just been thinking about how much better school would be if it were taught on a river and here I was, already getting bored with the long answer to a question that I asked on my own out of pure curiosity.

Tyson laughed too when I told him. Then he kept going on about how it was important to remember that something can always go wrong. I interrupted him, "But then again, that holds true with everyday life."

"Exactly!"

And the way he said it I knew that he wasn't trying to scare me about all the dangerous things in this world, but rather stress the importance of understanding and respecting them without succumbing to fear. Then he wrapped up the lesson repeating his original answer, "There is a time and place for everything."

I laughed and told him that didn't really apply to what we were talking about. All he said was, "I see. Let me know when you understand that it does." Then he chuckled again and we loaded into our rafts.

3:15 pm: We eddied out to take a break and scout out the final rapid. The weather is perfect today, and we hit lots of smaller rapids with flawless execution. Anna, our river guide is impressed with how well we are all working together in the boat.

I wished we had more time on the river.

3:45 pm: We finished scouting the rapid. The river gets narrower in this part of the canyon. Only twenty-five feet wide with tall cliffs on either side. Right in the middle of the rapid is this giant boulder that looks like a VW Beetle, but bigger. Then there is a ledge with a four foot drop on the other side. The rapid is called "Slug Bug." I hope Sarah isn't freaking out.

Anna explained to us that the key was to paddle straight for the boulder, and hit it dead on, bouncing off of it to the left side and on down to the drop. If you tried to paddle around the boulder you risked the chance of the boat wrapping itself around the rock and flipping. Sarah grabbed me by the arm when she heard the worst case scenario and I made her a promise I wasn't sure I would be able to keep. That everything was going to be fine.

When we got back to the boat Anna asked me if I would sit in the front. It is kind of a big deal to sit in the front of the boat. You have to be good at paddling because everyone else is following your lead. I told her that I would, so long as Sarah could be right behind me. On the other side in the front was Matt, the natural leader who could handle anything. I was honored to be in the same position as him. Especially since Steve and Allen kept congratulating me. They were so excited for me. For everything really.

We pulled the boat back into the river and hopped in, ready for anything. The familiar noise of gravity amplified with each paddle stroke until I could see the VW boulder dead ahead and the sound of the river maxed out to just below deafening. But as our focus sharpened for the task ahead, the noise of the river seemed to drown itself out, and my ears only heard what they needed to: the commands being shouted from Anna in the back of the boat.

With ten feet to go we braced for impact. We were lined up perfectly and when the rubber nose made contact, everyone lurched forward and found themselves caught off guard by the magnitude of the hit. Then came more shouts.

"RIGHT SIDE BACK PADDLE! LEFT SIDE FORWARD PADDLE!"

A short pause.

"DIG! DIG! DIG!"

And as we transformed her words into action the boat swung around so that it was facing directly upstream as we dropped over the final ledge. Backwards.

"HOLD ON! YE-HAWWWW!"

And just like that the water was calm again. As for us, we were anything but. Screams of success and smiles were exchanged by all.

Anna was ecstatic as she hollered, "I bet you guys didn't know what to do when we hit that drop backwards, did ya? I like to keep that last part a secret till the very end. Great work you guys, NOW GIVE ME FIVE STROKES FORWARD!"

4:30 pm: Having mastered the final rapid, the only thing that remained was to load up the boats onto a trailer that was waiting about a half mile downstream. We are driving back to the rafting company's headquarters for a well-deserved celebration.

We got to stay in the rafting company's bunk house that night instead of at a campground. Boys in bunks in one room and girls in another. And there were showers! After cleaning up I snuck off to meet up with Sarah down by the river while we waited for Tyson to get back. He had to hitch a ride to pick up our van upriver where we left it at the start of the river trip.

Sarah and I kissed for a long time. Then, when I suggested that it was time to head back, she told me that there was something she wanted to do. Said she didn't know if we would get another chance to take a shower for the rest of the trip and that she wanted to, you know.

Just then Lucy called our names. Tyson was back and everyone had been looking for us. We both felt guilty as hell as we walked past Lucy, even though nothing had happened. Still, it was awkward for all three of us until Lucy stopped me right before we were back and whispered, "I knew she liked you. Congratulations."

"Uh, it's not like that," I started, trying to play it off like it didn't mean that much to me.

But Lucy could read right through me. She giggled and said, "Well I think you two would make a great couple. Just be good to her, alright? She deserves it."

I would have never thought things would work out between me and Sarah, but Lucy was right, I did really like her. And she liked me too. She'd been really attached to me ever since "Granny's Washing Machine," but I didn't mind. I kind of liked it. Which was weird because I would have never guessed that in a million years. I promised Lucy I would take care of Sarah and then Lucy added, "You deserve it too Kris."

I think it was the nicest thing anyone's ever said to me.

DAY THIRTY:

10 am: Today we are just relaxing at the bunkhouse. Our only job is to wash our laundry and clean out the van. The rest of the day is for relaxing and resting up for our final backpack.

Steve and Allen had been going on and on throughout the entire trip about how they couldn't wait for the last backpack. How we would get to do a section of it on our own. I'd never given it much thought, but suddenly found myself kind of nervous about it. Mostly about what it would be like to be on my own in the middle of nowhere. I asked our river guide Anna if she had ever done anything like that before.

Of course her answer was yes, "I do a three day solo trip every year for my birthday," she explained, "Nothing clears your mind better than being isolated for a few days."

"Don't you ever get scared?" I asked.

"Oh hell yeah it can get scary out in the wild by yourself. That's the whole point. If you can accept that fear and then overcome it you can learn a lot about yourself. Hell, that's the problem with most people; they've never even spent a single day on their own in their whole lives. You know, truly isolated with no one around to impress. A lot can happen when you are on your own. I'd say I usually grow more in those few days on my own than the whole rest of the year combined. You know what I mean?"

But I didn't.

She was right. I never had gone a day without any human interaction. In a way she made me feel better about the thought of my upcoming time alone in nature. She didn't make me feel any less nervous about it, just more curious I guess. That was the thing about Anna, she didn't sugarcoat things. Just prepared you for them.

I ended up talking to her about a lot of stuff that afternoon. For some reason it was easy to talk to her. Maybe because she didn't know my whole story. Or because I knew I'd probably never see her again. But I felt like I could say anything and she wouldn't judge me. Or lie to me either. She was always straight up, and although it was intimidating at times, I liked it.

6 pm: After a lazy day on the banks of the river our guides cooked us one final feast. A rack of ribs. Moose ribs! They were delicious. One of the guides was also a hunter and killed a male moose the week before. We ate around a massive fire and listened to the guides tell stories about past trips and close calls.

Those guides up in Alaska were the real deal, no question about it. Especially Anna. They were by far the most impressive people I had ever met.

9:30 pm: Tonight's meeting was different than usual. The girls stayed in their room and we stayed in ours for a boy's only meeting. Tyson led it and we mostly just asked questions about all the things in life we shouldn't miss out on. Tyson was surprisingly honest with us. Every day he manages to gain more of my respect.

After our meeting, Tyson left and we stayed up talking about typical guy stuff. You know, sports, cars, but mostly sex. Who had done what. I think everyone lied, I know I did. I almost told them about me and Sarah, but I decided not to. It just didn't seem right.

We farted as loud as we could. We acted like men. It was glorious. And then it happened. Completely unintentionally, Jeff joked how one of the girl river guides looked "downright rapable."

An awkward laughter filled the room and then silence. All I could think about was Lucy. What had happened. What she asked me to do for her.

"That's not funny Jeff." I was almost shaking I was so nervous as the words exited my mouth.

"C'mon Kris, you know I was just joking."

"I know," and I tried to say it in a way so that he knew that I understood. Then I continued, firmly, "But it isn't funny. And I don't think you should keep joking about things like that when you go back home. None of us should."

It was dead quiet for a long time. Then Matt spoke up, "Kris is right, we hurt people all the time and we don't even know it."

No one was making eye contact, but everyone understood.

It was quiet for a long time, until Paul let out a fart that sounded painful. "Sorry guys, my bad."

Good old Paul, he always knew how to lighten the mood. Matt pulled me aside later that night and thanked me for saying something to Jeff. "I know standing up for someone else can sometimes feel like the hardest thing in the world. But you did good. Thanks Kris."

He was right. It was tough, especially because Jeff was my friend. But still, I was glad I did it. It needed to be done, and if I didn't say something, I doubt anyone else would have.

DAY THIRTY-ONE:

10 am: Leaving the river behind this morning was harder than I thought it was going to be. Something happened to me on the water. For the first time in my life I felt a true connection to nature. I was finally beginning to understand why Andrea chose to spend her summers up here. Why Tyson was so fond of the wilderness. Because it is wild and free. Perhaps that is why people like Andrea and Tyson feel so at home in it. Nature is the only place they can truly be themselves.

After saying our goodbyes to Anna and the rest of the river guides, we piled in the van and are headed north towards Denali National Park for our final backpack. But first we have to find a grocery store and resupply.

It was a long drive before we came across anything that remotely resembled a town with a grocery store. Andrea spent the van ride preparing individualized shopping lists for each of us. But instead of just listing items, she made it like a scavenger hunt with clues about the things we each needed to collect. She promised a big prize for whoever could correctly identify and find all of their items first and bring them to the front cashier where she and Tyson would be waiting.

The sleepy little town didn't know what hit them when we pulled up. All twelve of us piled out of the van and ran inside the grocery store, terrorizing the local shoppers with laughter and our disregard for normalcy. Everyone dressed in as goofy an outfit as they could muster up; Allen was wearing neon tights he borrowed from Jennifer, and Jennifer wore her pajamas. Everyone got into it. And then there was Paul. He just put his sleeping bag on over his head. There was a zipper at both ends of his bag and he opened the one where his feet usually belonged just enough to be able to see out of, even though no one could see his face inside. He kept bumping into everything and couldn't grab anything, let alone see his shopping list, because his sleeping bag lacked the necessary armholes, although I am sure he would have cut some if he had access to a pair of scissors.

Each of us grabbed a cart and took off scavenging the aisles. The locals didn't know what to do. I'm sure they had never seen anything like it before. It felt liberating to not worry at all what they thought and act crazy for our own personal benefit. I would have never even participated in something like this back home, but I was having the time of my life now. It is amazing how good it feels to let yourself go sometimes.

I used to let myself go back home, but it was different. I would do things like break a window or fantasize about hurting someone. You know, dark stuff. Lashing out like that was all I thought there was, the only way I knew how to vent. But no matter what I did, I never really felt better afterwards. It only felt good in the moment.

Behaving like that in the grocery store was so different. It allowed me to vent in a new way that lasted much longer and didn't end with me feeling guilty for my actions. I know it sounds crazy, but I was beginning to understand that there was more than one way to vent all the awkward energy, the pent up emotions of growing up. There were all sorts of ways, ways that didn't have to hurt anyone. Most of all myself.

Of course no one warned the manager of the store that this was just some kids having fun. He immediately freaked out; convinced we were a wild band of hooligans about to loot his store. Andrea and Tyson worked damage control with him while we ransacked the place. The contest wasn't even close, Lucy won by ten minutes easy. The rest of us eventually finished, except of course for Paul. We found him in the deli department. The only item in his shopping cart was his sleeping bag. He abandoned his list when the deli clerk asked him if he wanted to sample anything. He then proceeded to systematically try every type of meat and cheese they had. He was on to the multiple varieties of potato salad when we found him, and it was clear he was in sheer bliss. The rest of us took care of his shopping list and by the time we loaded back in the van he was sick to his stomach.

The rest of the van ride was filled with loud music and pure energy. When we pulled up to the campground right next to the trailhead for our final backpack the ranger knew she was going to have her hands full. She put us in the furthest spot away from anyone else and must have reminded us ten times about the campground's quiet hours policy. Tyson assured her we would be on our best behavior, but she could see right through him.

The ranger also made a huge deal about food. Nothing with a scent, not even toothpaste or Chap Stick could be left out overnight or stored in the tents. Everything with its own smell needed to be locked away because of the bear problem. She stressed the issue because a grizzly was seen in the campground the night before. Tyson instantly corrected her with, "Don't you mean a *brown bear*?"

She couldn't understand why the rest of us were laughing at his comment, but her seriousness of the situation sobered us up real quick. We set up camp constantly checking over our shoulders, convinced a grizzly might attack at any moment.

I was on cook crew for dinner and we were making a pasta dish to load up on carbs for the next day's hike. Tyson and Andrea were busy making more of their famous trail mix, and Paul kept meandering into the kitchen area. There was a very strict rule that no one was allowed in the kitchen area except for the cook crew during meal preparation. But Paul was on a mission. When we weren't looking he swiped something from the table and ran over to the campfire Jeff and Steve were working on. Jeff loved building fires. We all did, but Jeff was by far the best at it.

A few minutes later I glanced over and witnessed Paul pouring hot sauce directly into the fire.

"Paul," I screamed, "What the hell do you think you are doing?"

He looked up, innocent as a lamb with complete sincerity and casually replied, "I don't know, I was just seeing if this hot sauce would make the fire any hotter."

It was a completely logical hypothesis as far as he was concerned. Never mind that we were in bear country. Never mind that, well, never mind. I caught myself chuckling in the same way that Tyson did before asking Paul to return the hot sauce to the kitchen area, which he reluctantly did. He was so strange, and yet, like I said before, there was something that I couldn't help but appreciate about him. As I returned to my cooking duties I watched as Paul repeatedly tried to break into a bag of marshmallows for a pre-dinner treat. Paul loved marshmallows.

Tyson would catch him in the kitchen area and tell him to leave; only to find Paul underneath the van a few minutes later, rolling his way towards the bag of marshmallows. Once that attempt failed, Paul began to camouflage himself and hid from bush to bush trying to get close enough to the marshmallows without Tyson noticing. Each attempt was more comical and outlandish than the last, and what should have been annoying was somehow endearing.

Eventually, Tyson was distracted enough with something else, and Paul was able to acquire his treasure. When we called dinner and everyone gathered around, Paul was the last to arrive. He waddled over with a half empty bag and marshmallow residue all over his face. "Tyson," he confessed—as if it wasn't already obvious what happened—"I have to tell you something."

Tyson had a strange look across his face while he waited with anticipation for what Paul was about to say. "Well you see, I know you told me not to eat the marshmallows before dinner because I would just upset my stomach and ruin my appetite, but... they were right there, and... and you were busy with the ranger, and... and I saw the marshmallows, so I grabbed the marshmallows, and then I ate the marshmallows, and now... well, now I don't feel very good, and… and I know you were right, and I'm really sorry and all, but… now I know and I promise I won't do it again, so here… here are the marshmallows back. You're welcome, I mean thank you, I mean, uh…."

Then he popped another marshmallow in his mouth without even realizing it. All any of us could do was watch with bewilderment. That was Paul. That was our Paul, and you had to love it.

6:15 pm: After dinner we went over the maps for our backpack and this time I paid attention. I wanted to know as much as I could about where we were going and how to navigate on my own. Tomorrow is sort of like a test for us. We will be on the trail without the leaders. They'll hike up ahead of us. How well we do will determine how intense our solos will be. That's where we go off on our own and have to find our way back or something. I'm not really sure because they won't tell us too much about it yet. But I am trying to learn as much as I can now with hopes that they give me the chance to prove myself to them.

I told Tyson how I felt and waited for his usual chuckle. He didn't let me down before adding, "The task is an opportunity to prove to yourself what you are capable of. I am well aware of your potential Kris. I just hope that you are too."

His words meant a lot to me. I wanted to hug him, but I didn't, and then the moment passed.

8:30 pm: Our meeting tonight was quick and we are all going to bed early. It is going to be a long day tomorrow and we need as much rest as we can get. I never thought

I would be excited to go backpacking, but the back country has found a new ~~friend looking~~ soul searching for adventure.

Andrea came by to see if I was alright since I was the last one to go to bed. "Writing in your journal?" she asked.

I nodded.

"That's good. It seems like you are taking it much more seriously. Anything you'd be willing to let me read?"

"I don't know. Maybe later. They are kind of personal."

She looked disappointed so I added, "But you're right, the entries are getting longer. It's getting easier to write too. Who would have thought something like this could help me."

"How so?"

"Uh, you know, express myself I guess."

"Well I am glad to hear it Kris. Get a good night's sleep, alright?"

I told her I would. After she left I looked back at how lame some of my early entries were. I wanted to tear them out, but knew I couldn't change the past. I decided to focus on the ones to come instead.

DAY THIRTY-TWO:

9 am: Lucy's prize for winning the food shop scavenger hunt was a giant chocolate bar which she ended up sharing with the rest of us in the van ride yesterday. But the real prize is that she gets to be today's Leader-of-the-day. It is a big deal because we will be on our own and she is in charge.

After giving Lucy a map and showing all of us where we are trying to get to, Tyson and Andrea hiked up ahead while we finished getting ready. They were going to hike to our campsite, which was about seven miles away. They explained that if there were any parts of the trail that were questionable as to which way to go, they would mark the proper direction with a stack of rocks. It's called a cairn. Fortunately, the trail was supposed to be much more established than it was on our first backpack.

And just like that, Andrea and Tyson were gone. We were completely on our own.

We took our time getting ready, and finally got onto the trail about an hour and a half behind them. There was something empowering about us being on our own. Don't get me wrong, both Tyson and Andrea had grown on me a lot, but being on our own had a feeling of importance to it. We were responsible for not only ourselves, but for each other.

12 pm: It is a beautiful day, and we can see Denali off in the distance covered in snow. Most people know it as Mt.

McKinley, the tallest mountain in North America. But all the locals call it Denali which Andrea told us means "The High One" in one of the native languages, so that's what we call it too.

I spent most of the time up front with Lucy and Steve. She would show us the map and ask us where we thought we were on it. She was pretty good at reading it herself, and I think she was just being nice and wanted to include us.

2 pm: Lucy is doing a good job of taking enough breaks, but not too many. For a long time we hiked along the edge of this huge lake that was crystal clear. You could see the reflection of the mountains on the surface and it looked like a photograph that had been photo-shopped.

Imagine that, a place that is so real it looks fake. I could barely tell where the water ended and the tree line started in some areas on the other side. We decided to stop for a late lunch out on top of this tall peninsula with a perfect view of it all in an attempt to absorb what we were experiencing: the art of nature.

Out of nowhere Jeff announced that it was all too much and that he needed to swim in the masterpiece. It was warm out and a swim sounded refreshing. The only problem was that none of us packed a bathing suit. The girls didn't want to see any of the boys naked so they decided to hang out on the east facing shore of the peninsula while us boys went skinny dipping on the west side.

All of the boys were excited except for Matt. He didn't admit it, but you could tell he didn't feel comfortable getting naked in front of the rest of us. Jeff called him a fag and we all teased him till he unwillingly agreed. Our plan was to swim to a small island

and back, but halfway to it I heard a cry for help. It was Josh. Scrawny little Josh was pale as a ghost and it looked like he was about to drown. The water was cold, but manageable for the rest of us. But since Josh was all skin and bones he was struggling. Not only did he not have any body fat to help keep him afloat, but he was quickly becoming hypothermic from the frigid water. Matt was right next to him and Steve yelled for Matt to help. To all of our surprise, Matt said no. "He can make it back," Matt insisted, "Come on Josh, you can make it back on your own. You can do this."

But it was clear that Josh would drown before ever making it back on his own.

By now everyone was yelling at Matt to help. Matt was by far the strongest swimmer and it didn't make any sense why he wouldn't help. Everyone was panicking. Allen yelled, "Jesus Christ Matt, quit being such a goddamn homophobe and get over there and grab Josh before he drowns!"

Matt finally grabbed Josh by the arm and towed him back to shore. Jeff got his lighter from his backpack and made a small fire for Josh to warm up by. We stood around; waiting in our dry underwear while the sun robbed our bodies of the tingling sensation the water was all too happy to provide.

"What the hell was wrong with you out there Matt?" Steve demanded.

Josh could tell that tensions were high and couldn't help but feel responsible. He tried to calm everyone down by joking with Matt, "Yeah, what the hell man, it's not like I'm gay or anything. What did you think, I just wanted us to rub our naked bodies together or something?"

Lyle chimed in too, "I knew it. I knew you were gay Josh. And *this* is how you decided to hit on one of us?"

Josh joked back, "I'm not gay. You're the fag, not me."

Then Lyle said in a feminine voice, "No, you're the fag."

Everyone laughed and the mood began to relax. Everyone except for Matt. Out of nowhere he lashed out, "What the hell is wrong with you guys anyways? Always making gay jokes."

"Sorry," Lyle offered up, "I was just trying to make a joke. We all know Josh isn't really gay."

"Yeah, well what if he was?" Matt was livid.

"But he isn't."

"I'm not, I swear guys." Josh exclaimed.

Then Matt yelled, "Well I am, alright. And I hate how casually you all use someone *being gay* as an insult!"

Matt instantaneously realized the possible repercussions of his disclosure. His face filled with vulnerability.

Silence.

I couldn't believe it. Not in a million years. He didn't act at all like... like what I always thought gay people acted like. His confession threw my entire perception of gay stereotypes out the window.

Maybe because it was just us boys, or maybe because we had all become so close as a group over the course of the trip and viewed Matt as our unspoken team captain, our response was very different than what he feared it might be.

Instead, we were mostly just surprised and curious. All of us asked a bunch of questions. If he had ever told anyone, how he knew, stuff like that. I was waiting for someone to become uncomfortable with his honesty, to snicker and attack such a self-exposed target. But we as a group, collectively, were bigger than that sort of thing that afternoon.

Of all the questions we asked, the main one we wanted to know was why he never told anyone else before.

So he told us why. It was so simple. So sad.

"I never said anything because I was scared of how it would affect my life. I never felt like any of my friends back home would understand and look at me the same. Continue to believe in me. Stand up for me. Every time someone says something is 'gay' or calls someone a 'fag' it tears me apart inside. But I never, never once, told someone not to say it. I was so afraid that they would figure it out, that they would know and then look at me different. That's why I was scared of helping Josh."

Allen was the first one to say something. "Not now Matt. Not here. Not us."

Then Steve added with a smile, "You look the same to me Matt."

We all agreed. Paul, surprising eloquently, chimed in, "Yeah, you are still my idol Matt."

"Even more so now." Allen added.

And Matt began to smile a little. A feeling of relief overtook him. He told us he almost *came out* the night I stood up for Lucy in the bunk house. "I knew I could trust you guys then," he said, "But it is easier said than done. I have wanted to do that for so long. Admit to the world, to myself, who I am. I just can't believe it came out like this."

"You mean you can't believe that *you* came out like this," Jeff said trying to make light of all that just happened. He laughed. We all did.

I thought about how I had called just about every part of the beginning of our trip "gay." I called Lyle a "faggot" right before our fight. Hell, I was pretty sure I called everyone a "fag" at one point or another. And I had done so after making my promise to Lucy too. I never even thought about it like that. But I knew this was the same thing she was talking about. I felt terrible. I tried to apologize.

Matt reached over to give me a hug. And my instant reaction was to pull away, which made me feel even worse, but a lifetime of hateful programming can't always be dismantled that quickly. Because of my hesitation, he sat back down. His body language translated his humiliation crystal clear.

And in that split second I understood what Tyson meant on our first back-pack when the two of us scouted out a place to cross the creek. When he said, "Everyone has issues that they are dealing with. I don't care how good someone's life looks on paper; everyone has legitimate struggles from time to time."

I instantly jumped up and reclaimed the opportunity to make things right, tackling Matt to the ground, giving him the biggest hug I could. Everyone followed suit and dog piled on top. When it was over, tears were flowing from Matt's eyes.

Allen tried to console him, "Don't cry Matt, it's okay. It's going to be okay. You don't have to cry."

I wondered why people always say that. Why we tell people to stop crying. I mean, I know why we say it, because we relate crying with pain and we just want the ones we care about to be in as little pain as possible. But sometimes, sometimes the thing we need most is to let it all out. Instead of someone telling us to bury our emotions we just need a shoulder to cry on. Someone to say that it is okay to cry. Because it is a release of so much more than just tears. "Matt," and I looked directly in his eyes as I said, "It's okay to cry. It is okay to cry."

The girls finally met back up and confessed that they went skinny dipping too. They were surprised with our lack of excitement. None of us said anything about what happened. We figured that sort of thing was Matt's call, not ours.

6:30 pm: After a long day of hiking and blisters, we finally saw smoke and Andrea and Tyson's tent off in the distance. Our spirits soared as they greeted us with a warm meal already prepared. It felt good to see them again.

I wanted to tell them about the day, but it wasn't my place. Matt looked happier than ever, as if a huge weight had been lifted from his shoulders. But something didn't add up. This backpack was at a much higher elevation than we ever got to on our first backpack. And yet Matt was running around like it was no problem at all. I pulled him aside and asked him about that day from our first backpack when he and I both got sick just before summiting the peak by the saddle. He refused to admit that he was faking it. Instead he just smiled and said, "Solidarity Kris, solidarity."

It astounded me that he was willing to stick up for me without even knowing me back then. In fact, the only thing he did know about me was how "gay" I thought everything was. Regardless, he didn't seize the opportunity to turn my weakness into a form of vengeance through humiliation. Instead he stood up for me. And I knew that was the kind of person I wanted to keep as a friend for the rest of my life, regardless of who he was attracted to.

DAY THIRTY-THREE:

6:30 am: I wish I could sleep more but I am wide awake. Jeff is on cook crew and he made a bunch of noise getting up. Now I am cold and bored, just laying here.

All of a sudden there came the sound of chaos from outside the tent. Next thing I knew, Allen stumbled past mumbling, "He killed it. I can't believe he killed it."

I couldn't see anything through the tent and had no clue what was happening. Killed what? Steve and I threw on some clothes and rushed out of the tent to see what happened.

I scanned the campsite and found no dead bodies in sight. In fact, the only two people up were Allen and Jeff, and Jeff seemed happy as could be. He was laughing as he played with what looked like a marionette puppet. Upon closer inspection it became increasingly evident that his marionette was in fact a dead mountain dog.

You see, there are these animals that look just like small prairie dogs up here. Except the habitat we are in is anything but a prairie. It is mountainous tundra. So Allen classified them as mountain dogs, a distant relative of the prairie dog.

By now everyone else was up, and an investigation was underway. Jeff couldn't control his laughter as he teased Allen that the ordeal was his fault, despite the fact that Allen was a vegan who considered himself a protector of animals. Allen didn't even try to fight the claim.

What happened was Jeff and Allen woke up early to get breakfast going. A mountain dog kept on trying to steal some of the food. They can be a real nuisance. Jeff was whittling away at a stick with the knife he bought in Anchorage when Allen, frustrated with the mountain dog's persistence, casually suggested that Jeff

151

attempt to scare off the critter by throwing his knife at it. Jeff refused initially, afraid he might actually hit the small animal.

"Are you kidding me?" Allen laughed, "I bet you your next cook crew you couldn't hit that thing. Don't you see how quick they are?"

So Jeff took the bet, and with a thousand to one odds of hitting such a small creature from ten feet away, threw his knife. End over end the knife flew across the kitchen area until it miraculously found the target's chest, killing the defenseless animal almost instantly. Neither of them could believe it. While Allen freaked out and let a sense of guilt get the best of him, Jeff found two pieces of tall grass and tied slip-knots on the end of them. Anna had showed us this technique on the river and taught us how to catch lizards with them. But now, Jeff attached the tall grass around the front paws of the lifeless creature and proceeded to chase Allen around with it blaming him for its unnecessary death.

The whole thing was so strange and Tyson didn't know what to say, so Andrea said something none of us could believe.

"Alright boys, here's the deal: you kill it, you grill it."

She assured us that no living thing was going to die in vain on her watch, and that the only honorable thing to do was cook it up for breakfast. She reached into the first-aid kit and handed Jeff a pair of rubber gloves. That morning the boys all hovered over Jeff's shoulders while he attempted to skin his first ever kill. What originally disgusted us soon became an obsession, and although there was very little meat, we all claimed which part was ours. Five of us ended up trying it, and it really didn't taste like much of anything. I thought it would taste like chicken, because that's what people say most strange meat tastes like. But without any seasoning, it was rather bland.

Jeff swore that he was going to keep the hide and make a wallet out of it when he got home, promising to send it to Allen as a birthday gift in the fall. Allen still felt terrible about it all, though his curiosity got the best of him and he finally told Jeff that he would be disappointed if Jeff didn't keep his word.

2 pm: After an unusual breakfast, we hiked deeper into the back country. We just made it to the top of this huge pass. It was tough, but rewarding too. The view is unbelievable. Endless mountains in all directions. We are truly in the wild. We are free.

I was way up front from the rest of the group with Tyson and we waited for everyone else to catch up. We had been talking about how to make sure things would be different for me back home.

"Are you nervous about seeing that Cody kid at school next year?" he asked.

"Nah, not really. They decided I would be going to a new school next year. No one there is even supposed to know about anything that happened."

"Sounds like another second chance for you then."

"Yeah, I guess. It's just that, well, ah I don't know, forget it."

But Tyson wouldn't let it go, "What is it?"

I waited a while. Tried to figure out what I was even trying to say. "It's just, I am really nervous that one of two things is gonna happen. Either the same thing that happened at my old school, where I get picked on every day, or something like what happened with Lyle. I mean let's face it, there are good kids, and then there are bad ones."

"No there aren't."

"Huh?"

"Look Kris, everyone has the potential to be a good person. I believe that," he was quiet for a minute, "Do you think you are one of the good ones or one of the bad ones?"

"I don't know. Both? Maybe?" I was still all over the place inside, trying to figure it all out. Sure I had been improving, but what if it didn't last? I wanted to be good, but had serious doubts about my personal character ever since what happened back home.

Tyson thought about it for a long time. "It is going to be tough Kris. You're right. I wish that wasn't the case, but it is. I think the key is to try to stay strong."

"But that's why the bullies picked on me in the first place. Because I was weak. How do you change that? You know, without becoming a jerk like I was for the first part of this trip."

"I don't know. Let me think about that for a while, okay?"

It killed me that he didn't have an immediate answer. For a minute there I thought he would. But deep down I knew that it wasn't that easy.

Finally he suggested, "I guess it might be best if you just try to fly under the radar for a while."

"But then what? I don't want to live my whole life under the radar."

"I think the key is to just be yourself Kris. People will like you when you aren't trying to be something you are not."

"But I…" I couldn't admit that I still had no clue who I was.

Tyson kept going, "I think everyone in the group can appreciate you for who you are now."

I was starting to feel sorry for myself, "Yeah, and who's that?"

"Well for one thing, you are a caring person. You jumped out of that raft after Sarah without even thinking about it."

His pep talk was finally starting to get to me. Unfortunately, the rest of the group began to appear and I asked if we could drop it till later. All Tyson said was, "I wouldn't worry if I were you. You will figure out who you are. You've already started to on this trip, you just might not realize it yet."

He was right and I knew it. I thought about how I had changed since the start of the trip over a month ago. But mostly, I thought about the ways I still wanted to change. Maybe I did have both good and bad in me. Maybe everyone does. But maybe if I kept focusing on the good parts, things would be okay back home.

8:15 pm: During our meeting tonight Andrea and Tyson congratulated us all on how well we were doing and announced that we were all ready for the solo activity they had been planning for tomorrow. We are all super excited and feel like we have earned it. I am just excited to prove myself. I hope that Anna was right, that a day on my own in nature will help me find myself better. I think I have come a long way, but I know I have a long ways to go.

DAY THIRTY-FOUR:

9 am: This morning we prepared for our individualized solo assignments. Andrea and Tyson explained to us how they would work. The two of them would remain at our current campsite while each of us headed out in a different direction to a pre-designated spot. Yesterday evening they placed personal notes in plastic Easter eggs out in the wilderness for each of us to try and find. The difficulty of the placement of each note depended on how well they thought each of us could handle the challenge.

They handed each of us a compass and set of instructions. Once we find our note we can return to the campsite. Of course anyone can come back sooner if they want, whether finishing the task or not. The only other rule is that all of us need to return by 8pm tonight. I am ready for this challenge!

Sarah asked if we could meet up during our solos, but completing this challenge meant a lot to me, and I hoped that Andrea and Tyson gave me one of the more challenging tasks.

1 pm: I am taking a quick lunch break. This morning, after an inspiring pep talk from Andrea, I set my compass to 282 degrees North, Northwest and set off looking for a tree that had been struck by lightning some half mile away. From there, I needed to find a giant boulder twenty degrees to the north. It's been going on

like this all day. It's much more difficult than I thought it would be, which in a way keeps me going because it reminds me that Andrea and Tyson must have really believed I could handle it.

At first I would catch glimpses of the rest of the group, but soon there was a feeling of isolation. Peace. It was nice to spend the time alone. I was used to spending short stints of time alone back home, but this was different. I had no idea what challenges and experiences were waiting for me. All I knew was that if I did come across any problems, it would be up to me to solve them. Sure, we were all given whistles in case of an emergency, but I swore to myself I wouldn't let it come down to that. I was so confident, in fact, that I left mine back at our base camp.

2 pm: I'm stuck on one of the directions. I was supposed to find this burnt out log but I've been looking for almost an hour. I swear the thing doesn't exist. I finally found a log that looks like it might have been struck by lightning so I am setting my compass for the next item.

I found myself beginning to rationalize very loose interpretations of the landmarks written out for me until it was more than obvious that I was nowhere near where I needed to be. I wondered if anyone else was having problems, if anyone else had made it back yet. I hoped that they didn't make things too difficult for Paul. Then I hoped that they didn't make things too difficult for me.

I tried to retrace my steps. I knew the general direction our camp was because of my compass, but refused to return to the group empty handed. My frustration transformed into distraction and soon it was starting to seem like I was completely lost. I didn't know what to do. A light drizzle developed, but it was nothing I was too worried about. Instead I focused on orienting myself and finding my way back to an earlier landmark. One that I knew was right.

Andrea talked about getting lost in the woods. How easy it was and how important it was to stay where you were. But I didn't have time for that. Besides, without a whistle, what good would it have done? And I still hadn't admitted to myself that I was truly lost. So I just wandered aimlessly looking for something recognizable.

Soon the drizzle turned to rain. I put on my rain gear, but it was already too late. My inner layer had soaked through. As the cold front moved in the temperature began to drop dramatically. I began to shiver and knew I needed to keep moving. I tried to ignore the reality that I had naïvely put myself in a very dangerous position, which only made things worse.

5:30 pm: I am lost.

I know what you are probably thinking. Why not just go back the way I came? But all the trees really did start to look the same after a while. I walked in circles till I couldn't tell what I'd seen and what I hadn't.

By the time I was ready to admit to myself that I made some very serious errors, it was too late. I began to understand that something far more pressing than my pride was at stake. My survival.

And then I saw him. Way off in the distance, a grizzly came into my view. Fear consumed whatever thoughts were previously focused on how cold I was. Fortunately I was upwind from him, and he didn't seem to notice me. But I was out in the wide open and there wasn't anything close to take cover behind. All I could do was sit patiently and wait till he exited the scene.

I was impressed with the grizzly we saw at the zoo, but seeing one out in the wild was an entirely different experience. The bear at the zoo looked defeated. As if it was just killing time. The bear that stood two hundred yards in front of me resembled neither of these qualities. He walked confident and proud, as if he knew how spectacular of a creature he was. I found myself mesmerized by his stride. The way he took his time moving across the landscape, occasionally shaking the rain from his fur. He was a true master of his environment. And although I should have been more terrified, I found myself in complete appreciation of the opportunity.

Slowly but surely, he disappeared from my vision. As soon as he did my senses came back with a vengeance. The rain had let up by now, but I was freezing, and I knew my fate rested solely in my hands.

There were two options really. Keep moving till I found my way back to camp or try to make a fire to combat the inevitable hypothermia that would soon set in.

I tried to stay as level headed as possible, differentiating between perceived risks and real ones. I knew both options involved very real risks, and focused on making a calculated decision.

I'd already eaten the food I brought for the day, and knew that my energy levels would only continue to drop. If I kept moving and didn't make my way back soon enough I would collapse from exhaustion and then be at the mercy of the elements. In other words, I could realistically die cold and alone in the middle of nowhere.

On the other hand I could try to do something about my body temperature. I knew this would be easier said than done. I didn't have my lighter on me. I gave it to Paul to use in case he needed it. Funny how life works sometimes. There was of course another way to make a fire.

I could bust an open flame.

I knew I had to accept how difficult the task of starting a fire by hand would be. But more importantly, I knew that if I was to attempt it, to really try, it would only be possible with a hundred percent commitment. Not just physically, but mentally as well.

Busting would require all the remaining energy I had. If I failed, the consequences would be the same as with the first option. A lonely death in the middle of nowhere.

But there was a key difference between the two options. If I tried to find my way back, I would need to rely on a certain degree of luck that I would blindly stumble across something distinct that I would recognize from before getting lost. However, because I had the knowledge base to bust, the only thing I needed to rely on to start a fire was my own ability. Luck was far less of a factor. After calculating all possible outcomes, the decision was clear.

6:45 pm: I will start a fire to keep from freezing to death.

The first step was to prepare myself mentally. I thought of Anna, and her ability to focus on making the best out of whatever situation she found herself in rather than becoming overwhelmed by mistakes of the past. I reminded myself that this time failure was not an option, and more importantly that I was capable of the task at hand.

I began to feel a wave of confidence come over me and searched for some dry wood. Despite the rain, I found plenty of dry willow under shrubs and bushes. Next I looked for a place that was as protected from the wind as possible. I compiled all the supplies I would need and began to prepare a fire board and spindle. I wished I had bought a knife when everyone else did in Anchorage so that I could sharpen the end of my spindle, but made do without. I remembered when I acknowledged that the odds of ever really needing a knife were one in a million. I tried to laugh about it rather than dwelling on something that could not be changed. I pushed on and sharpened the spindle against a rock. I used one of my shoelaces for the bow string and was soon ready to start.

I took a deep breath, reviewed my strategy and visualized my success. Then I placed a smooth rock over the top of the spindle for friction, stepped on one side of the fire board, and began to slide the bow forward and back. With my first stroke forward the spindle dislodged itself from the rock and launched a good five feet. I reminded myself that such things were bound to happen, rubbed some extra grease from under my eyes onto the top of the spindle so that the friction was focused on the fireboard, and tried again.

I started to develop a groove almost immediately, and thought I created an ember within the first five minutes. But I stopped to check too soon and lost it. After that I didn't even come close for a good twenty minutes. As much as I tried to fight it I kept thinking about losing Sarah's hand in the rapid. I caught myself wondering if my best just wasn't good enough after all.

This type of thinking is dangerous because it has the ability to destroy the faith a person has in himself. The faith that is needed to be successful. It was starting to get the best of me. I allowed doubt into the equation. I wish I could say that wasn't the case but there wasn't much point in lying by that point. Exhausted and sore, I stood up and walked around to clear my head. I began to cry.

I was crying because I had always believed that there was no room for doubt if a person wanted to succeed at something. Doubt represented weakness, and weakness ensured failure. I thought about the heroes from the movies I watched growing up. Heroes who showed no weakness. And then it dawned on me that all those stories were nothing but lies. Bullshit. They had to be. It just couldn't be the case. That wasn't how it really worked. Not for most of us at least. Not for me.

And the more I thought about it the more upset I became at the fact that most of the people we worship in society aren't really heroes at all. There are plenty of reasons why they aren't, but most importantly because they are never fully honest with us or themselves. And these false heroes we look to for guidance have no clue how dangerous withholding their personal failures from us is. Because it instills in us that in order to succeed you must be without doubt at all times. And that is not human. Not human at all.

A true hero must end up second guessing their abilities from time to time, right? They must. And then I remembered Tyson. I thought about how he described his experience busting. How hard it was for him. He was the best hero I could ask for. He had always been honest with us about his triumphs and failures, stressing how it was alright to doubt oneself along the way. It was more than alright, it was natural.

I felt liberated by the epiphany. I dug deep. I accepted the doubts I had of success but refused to let them develop into fear.

So I picked up my self-made tools and continued to fail. Hours of failure compiled while doubt came and went, but I never lost hope. Every now and then I would create an ember, but could never successfully transfer it to my tinder nest. Still, I pushed on and was persistent with my failure until that failed too.

And out of the failure to fail came success. I carefully tapped an ember from the firebox and into my tinder nest made of dried out leaves and grass. The ember ignited the tinder nest with my first breath. I placed the tinder nest under my kindling and blew the strongest breaths I had left in me. Within a minute the flame was consistent and I carefully added wood to the fire that I had created from scratch.

As the heat rose from the ground and was absorbed by my body tears of joy flowed over the dried up salt of previous tracks. The tears of sadness were gone now and with them went something else. The part of me that believed everything all the bullies ever said, what I allowed myself to believe for far too long: that I was not good enough for this world.

My thoughts had never been so clear. I understood that I did far more than just start a fire with those sticks. Busting not only saved my life, it served as a rite of passage that brought instantaneous—yet hard earned—maturity and understanding with it. The insecurities I previously masked with a naive cockiness were no longer necessary, and were now replaced with a far more sustainable inner confidence. I proved to myself once and for all that I was able to be responsible for myself, that I was capable of anything, so long as I believed in myself. The secret was in the ability to acknowledge doubt without losing hope.

11:45 pm: I busted on my own. I made the fire huge. Jeff, our group pyro, would have been proud. So would Tyson. I am proud. I watch as the flames heal my body. In them I can see the hefty grizzly I witnessed earlier and all that he represented to me. Tonight, I too am a master of my environment.

I laughed at the fact that I didn't need a knife after all. Sure it would have helped, but if I could survive out here without one, I could definitely make it without one back home, too. And something inside of me knew that I was going to make it out of this ordeal alive. I made a plan and decided to try to get some sleep until the fire burnt itself out. It was after midnight by now. My body needed to rest and I figured that I would wake up feeling more energized. With a clear head I would carefully try to retrace my steps free from the rash decisions based on anxiety and frustration that plagued me before. Patience would be my secret to success.

1:30 am: I've been dozing in and out for the last hour or so, but never really passed out like I hoped I would. I keep imagining I hear my name being called, but it must just be the wind. At least the fire is still going.

And then I heard Tyson's chuckle, directly behind me.

I turned around as he casually said, "I hoped that was you."

"How did you find me?"

"The smoke from the fire. Isn't that why you made it?"

"Yeah. Actually, no."

I told him what had happened as he gave me some food. All of it. I waited for him to scold me for not putting on my raingear sooner, for getting lost, not bringing my whistle, for scaring the crap out of him and Andrea. But he didn't. I guess he could tell that I would never forget those sorts of lessons after what I'd gone through. The main thing he was interested in was how I got the fire started.

"No lighter? Nothing?"

I laughed. Then I added, "I could do it again for you if you'd like."

He chuckled to himself and patted me on the back as he confided in me, "Well, Kris, I am truly impressed. You have earned my deepest respect."

"How so? I screwed up so many ways in order to get here."

"True. But you managed to defy the impossible when it was absolutely necessary."

I thanked him for the compliment. Before getting some more rest I asked Tyson if I could lead on the way back to the campsite in the morning.

"Let's do it together," then he chuckled adding, "I'm a little turned around myself."

DAY THIRTY-FIVE:

8:15 am: Still alive and back with the group. Still tired, even though I slept much better once Tyson showed up. Tyson had brought food, water, and a space blanket for me. He built up the fire and we both decided to sleep before attempting to find our way back to the group. We woke up around five this morning, eager to reunite with the others. I couldn't believe how far I had gotten from our camp site.

On our way back I showed Tyson where I climbed a hill in search of a good overlook. He chuckled and explained that I walked a giant horseshoe and was way past where my egg was. He said we were going to take a more efficient route the rest of the way back. Sure enough, we arrived at our campsite in less than two hours.

When we showed up everyone freaked out. They all ran over to us with open arms and a million questions. Tyson told them to relax and give me some space. Andrea gave me some oatmeal to warm me up. Then everyone sat and listened while I told them what happened. I tried real hard not to exaggerate, or make myself out to be some sort of a hero or anything. They knew better by then anyways.

When I first shared my story with the rest of the group I was still a little bummed that I failed at accomplishing my original goal.

"But you succeeded at busting Kris," Steve pointed out, "and that is almost impossible."

Andrea spoke up, "I think that what happened out there is about a lot more than just failure and success. What do you think Kris?"

I was pretty sure I knew what she meant. "It was about growth, I think. Anna and I talked about this sort of thing when we were on the river."

"What do you mean?" Sarah asked.

So I tried to explain, "Well maybe personal growth is more important to focus on rather than the failures and successes that happen along the way."

Paul chimed in with a full mouth of trail mix, "Wait, isn't that what this trip is supposed to be all about. I swear I read something like that in the brochure."

We all laughed at how profound Paul's statement was despite him knowing it.

"You're right Paul," Lucy said, "That is exactly what this trip is all about."

"Not just this trip," I corrected her, "I think that is what life is all about too."

12:30 pm: After a nice little nap, everyone else told me about their solos. Each of them was convinced that theirs was the most challenging. Andrea and Tyson refused to admit who's really was. But everyone had completed their task. Except me, of course. Andrea tried to say it was her fault that I got lost, that she screwed up the instructions somehow. I thanked her for trying to make me feel better, but told her I was done trying to blame others for my problems.

I've spent my whole life doing that, blaming others, and it's never gotten me anywhere anyways. Normally I would have been happy, even desperate to blame someone or something else if I failed at something. But I was beginning to realize that there was more to it than that. Andrea was right, the traditional labels of *failure* and *success* didn't really belong with my experience.

We finished lunch and packed up. Then, together, we started to make our way out of the backcountry. We took it slow and enjoyed our time. I mostly stayed at the back of the group with Andrea and Paul.

9 pm: The moon is full this evening and we chose a campsite overlooking a lake. The sunset lasted for hours and the reflection of the clouds on the water was the perfect backdrop for our meeting. Steve and Allen begged me to tell about the grizzly and busting again. I was happy to share. In a way, it helped me process it all. Anna was right about how much could happen to you when you spent some time in the wilderness by yourself.

DAY THIRTY-SIX:

8 am: We packed up early and are headed back to the trail head. I'm making sure to try and take it all in, the scenery, the fresh air, all of it. And I'm trying to talk with as many people as possible. Hiking is the perfect way to get to know someone better.

The first person I tried to talk to on the trail was Lyle. It went okay. Nothing amazing though. I guess that's alright. It wasn't awkward or anything, we've both just kind of accepted our differences and do our own thing. Still, I tried to apologize for the day of the fight. He said it was no big deal and kept changing the subject so I eventually let it go. I figured that I tried, and that was all anyone could do sometimes.

I couldn't help but wonder if someone like Lyle got that much out of our trip. It didn't seem like it on the surface. But then again, that was exactly the type of assumption that kept me from understanding the rest of the group at the beginning of the trip when I wrote them all off just because I thought they were a bunch of rich brats.

I tried to think about Lyle as if he were an iceberg. I knew that there was a lot going on beneath the surface. Who knew, maybe he did get a lot out of our trip after all. I hoped so. I hoped there was more to him than just a rich prick. It was too bad he never opened up more.

Thinking about Lyle like that made me want to talk to Jennifer next. She was the first one that I jumped to conclusions about. We talked for a long time and I realized she wasn't really a bitch after all. She was just scared and confused like everyone else. I tried to tell her that acting like that didn't really help. I kind of waited for her to slap me for saying so. But I think she really thought about it. I hoped some of it got through to her. I found myself repeating

Tyson's advice to me when I told her she could be so much cooler if she didn't try so hard. I had to laugh.

I also had a long talk with Katie. She told me she already knew about me and Sarah. I asked her all sorts of questions trying to get some dirt on her sister. Katie was loving it and told me all sorts of funny stuff. Like how one time when they were little Sarah decided to cut all of her hair off. Katie promised she would send me a picture when we got back home.

4:45 pm: Nine miles later we are back at the trail head. Back at our van. The signs of civilization fill the group with a sense of excitement. But the return to the familiar brings with it a sense of sadness too. I know what it represents. And I am already finding myself longing for a return to nature. Only now as I am about to leave it behind can I truly appreciate and respect such wilderness.

I told Steve how I felt and he told me that he wet his sleeping bag on his very first trip like this. "I hated it," he confided, "because I was so scared of being outside and getting dirty. I even asked my leaders to send me home. I remember I couldn't wait for the trip to be over. But by the end, just like you, I was a new person. And look at me now, I am the king of dirt!"

He laughed as he smeared mud on his cheeks. We both laughed. Steve was a good guy. Then he let me play with his camera some more. He showed me photos from throughout the trip. I couldn't believe all that we had done.

8:30 pm: Tonight we are camping at the trail head. Tyson and Andrea surprised us by cooking dinner. Allen led the meeting and asked us to say something nice about the person to our left. For me that was Steve. I talked about what a great tent mate he was, and how he was always helping me out. How it meant a lot to me when he got so excited for me getting to be at the front of the boat on the river trip. And for teaching me about photography. But really, for teaching me the importance of finding my own creative outlets in life. For a second there I thought I was going to make him cry and he gave me a big old bear hug. It was one of my favorite meetings so far.

DAY THIRTY-SEVEN:

10 am: We started heading back to Anchorage this morning. Today is our last big drive day. Andrea told us it was a day to think about everything that has happened.

As people dozed off I held Sarah in my arms and we planned out fictitious trips to each other's houses. Trips that I hoped would happen, despite the obvious obstacles that stood in the way. I had no way to get to Vegas, and I doubted her parents would be very welcoming. Maybe Katie would be willing to drive her to California, but that seemed unrealistic too. And there was no way my family would even let them stay with us anyways. Still, it made me smile to picture a future rendezvous in my head. It made her smile too. That was the best part.

5 pm: We've been driving all day. Everyone ended up falling asleep to the music that Andrea put on. Hippy music from the sixties. I am tired too, but I can't stop thinking about everything that happened to me this summer. It's kind of overwhelming.

Andrea could tell I had a lot on my mind. Since I was pretty much the only one awake she asked if I had any music requests. I told her that her music was fine and that I liked it. She smiled and told me to let her know if I changed my mind.

8 pm: We stopped at a pizza place for dinner, but everyone was too tired to even enjoy it. When we finally pulled into our campground we begged to be left alone. But Tyson is insisting that we set up our tents and still have our meeting.

Josh suggested that our meeting should be a quick one. He pleaded his case, "Nothing really happened today so there isn't much to talk about anyways."

I knew he was right, but a part of me was disappointed. I was really starting to enjoy the meetings. Fortunately, Katie spoke up, "Look, we only have a couple of meetings left. As the Leader-of-the-day I am asking that we ALL try to make sure that we have a good one tonight."

9:45 pm: Unfortunately the group was just too tired for it to be a great meeting. Katie's question was a good one though. She asked each of us to talk about a fear that we overcame this summer. My answer was that I was no longer afraid of myself. I know what I am capable of, both the good and the bad. This summer I realized that I have to accept that I am capable of violent mood swings and outbursts. But more importantly, I know that I am capable of channeling the fears and insecurities that typically tend to trigger those eruptions into other outlets. Creative outlets rather than destructive ones.

See, all the violent and destructive outbursts that I used to think were the only way I could vent or express myself were always so short lived. And they only ended up with me feeling even worse than before. About myself. Life. Everything. But now I see that creating something, anything, is a far healthier outlet for the pain I feel inside. Creation brings more understanding and inner peace than destruction ever could.

I always knew the ways I lashed out in the past were wrong. The problem was I didn't care. I didn't know any other way. But of course there are lots of other ways. For me, this trip, this journal has introduced me to writing. Something I used to hate. But now I kind of like it. It's a way to express what's going on inside of me. Maybe with some practice I could write for a living in the future. Who knows?

I guess it all comes down to the fact that I can only expect to get out of life what I put in. I used to think that revolved around pain. The more I received, the more I justified passing pain on to others.

It is so freeing to understand that life doesn't have to be that way. In fact, there is no "one right way" to make it through this life.

The important thing is that I am starting to believe that I will make it.

DAY THIRTY-EIGHT:

10 am: I stayed up all night writing in my journal. ~~Luckily~~ Fortunately, we got to sleep in all morning long. The only thing we have to do today is clean all of our gear and then celebrate. Nobody's mentioned that it is our last full day together, they don't have to. The general mood has made it clear enough.

Before we could celebrate, everything had to be cleaned. The tents, stoves, van, everything. I was in charge of washing the tents and took pride in leaving them spotless for the next group who would be using them the following summer.

3:45 pm: We did such a good job cleaning that Andrea and Tyson offered to take us to a nice restaurant in town to celebrate the end of our trip. As tempting as it sounded, we decided we will cook for ourselves and have a campfire instead.

Lucy summed it up best, "We can eat at a restaurant any time we want back home. This is our last chance to cook together. To be together. And I'd rather spend the time where we belong: out here in the open air."

7:45 pm: We just finished a massive feast, and everyone helped out. Even Paul was happy to contribute to the preparation of the strawberry shortcake for dessert, which he must have eaten half of in the process. I was in charge of cutting up all the vegetables for the salad. It *was the best dinner I think I have ever had. Jeff and Matt are making a giant campfire for our final meeting.*

A few of us sat around the fire while the rest of the group got ready for the meeting. Katie asked, "Can you guys believe we've been away from our homes for almost forty days?"

No one could.

"So much has happened." Lucy said.

Paul pointed out, "Forty days seems like forever, but it went by so fast."

"I can't believe it is almost over." Allen shrugged, disappointed.

Matt asked, "Do you guys feel like you have changed at all?"

I knew I did, "I still can't believe how much happened in such a short time. It sounds impossible just thinking about it, but this summer has changed things for me forever. Saved me, from myself, mostly. Or at least, who I thought I was supposed to be. Saved my life."

The others agreed I had come a long way. It was a comforting feeling to know that they saw a change in me too. Then Andrea asked me to share a little more. "How so?" she asked.

I thought about it for a long time. Finally I offered up, "Well, for one thing, now I know who I am not."

"And who's that?" She pressed on.

I looked around the fire into the eyes of people who had slowly but surely become my friends over the course of the summer, "I am not a bully."

Andrea looked satisfied, but I kept going, "More important, I am not afraid. I am not afraid of the kids who picked on me back home, because I know most of them are just as confused as me."

Out of nowhere Steve confessed, "Don't worry Kris, you're not the only one who is awkward and unskilled at growing up."

"It's hard," Matt admitted.

"Yeah," Paul added, "A lot of the time it sucks."

"You're not alone Paul," Lucy said.

"None of us are," I said, "I guess that's my point. No one is. Everyone has their own issues they are dealing with."

Tyson looked at me and nodded. I nodded back. Then he asked, "So who are you?"

I stoked the fire before responding, "Well, I am still trying to figure that out. But what I do know—so far—is that maybe I am, or can be, a good person. You know, someone who will try to stand up for others, because I wish someone would have stood up for me when I was younger."

Lucy leaned over and gave me a hug. Then she whispered, "This summer wouldn't have been the same without you Kris. Thank you. I know you will do great."

Matt was the final Leader-of-the-day and before he asked us his question, I requested to say something. I told the group that I had a new answer to one of the daily questions from the beginning of the trip: "What's the hardest thing you have ever done?"

The first time the question was asked I made a joke out of it, disrespecting Tyson and Andrea in the process. That was before I started taking the meetings seriously. Everyone figured my new answer would be busting, the same as Tyson's. But it wasn't.

More specifically, more honestly, I modestly offered up my new answer to the group, "The hardest thing I have ever done in my life was to make the conscious decision to believe in myself."

Before making the commitment to bust I was always convinced my best was never good enough. The result was simple: a lack of action and commitment. Something was missing from the equation. Choosing to believe in myself was the key. Believing in myself was both the hardest and best thing that ever happened to me. It saved my life. Literally, it did.

I thanked everyone for giving me a second chance to answer, a second chance for the trip. The group thanked me for my honesty and the meeting went strong all night. No one wanted it to end, but one by one the group grew tired and retired to their tents.

11:30 pm: At tonight's meeting everyone wore a mix of emotions across their fire-lit faces. Sadness clashed with laughter, tears with smiles while we reminisced about all that had happened. Allen and Steve swore up and down that this was the best summer of their lives. I told them I agreed.

Before going to bed Sarah and I went for a walk. I took her to the log I smoked at the first day of the trip. I didn't have anything left to smoke by then anyways, but I didn't care. I was sure I would still do that sort of thing back home, I did like it after all. But drinking and smoking just to escape didn't sound as appealing anymore. I'd rather try that stuff for the experience itself, and the more you do it the less of an experience it becomes. Instead it just turns into a habit.

We kissed for a long time sitting on that log next to the river. I wanted to tell Sarah that everything was going to be fine for her, that she didn't need me anymore, but when I started to talk she stopped me. She told me that neither of us needed to say anything. Then she asked, "Do you have any…um…protection?"

I said no because I didn't.

I was in shock! I couldn't believe that was on the table. That she would have been down for that. I fumbled for an excuse, and asked if that was okay. "Of course it's okay that you don't have a condom on you out here in the wilderness!" As I started to unbutton my pants, she stopped me with, "but, we aren't going to have sex without one."

She said the last part with so much confidence, and I realized that she was stronger than I had given her credit for. Part of me wondered if she was even a virgin. If it really mattered. All I knew was that I was drawn to her confidence and the way she was so straight up about sex. About her requirements when it came to sharing her body with someone else.

Then she kissed me and I kissed her back. We got really close a couple of times, but in the end we didn't do it. The decision was hers and I knew I needed to respect it.

We held each other and promised to keep in touch once we got home. I wondered how long it would last. She told me she loved me. I told her I loved her too, and I think I do, but the truth of it is that I don't know the first thing about love. I wondered if that was what it felt like. I wondered about a lot of things as I held her in my arms making promises about the future, no matter how unrealistic they may have been.

DAY THIRTY-NINE:

4 am: Andrea woke us all up and we are headed to the airport.

I'd only gotten back to the tent about twenty minutes before that.

6:15 am: Jennifer, Lyle and Josh were the first to go, and were gone before any of us even realized it. Now there is a long wait at the airport till the next group of people go.

While we waited, some people offered confessions from the trip. Most of it was pretty silly stuff. Like Jeff secretly putting some of his gear in Matt's backpack so Jeff had a lighter load to carry. Allen told us that he had kissed Jennifer, but everyone already knew that.

I didn't mention anything about me and Sarah. Part of me wanted to brag about it, but it just didn't seem appropriate.

And then there was Paul. He had all sorts of confessions. But my favorite one was about his trail mix. Like I said before, the trail mix Andrea and Tyson made for us was probably the best trail mix ever in the history of mankind. So much so that a few people confessed to stealing handfuls from each other's bags when no one was looking. Paul was guilty of that too, but his confession was that he was so afraid of other people taking his trail mix that he would sleep with it under his pillow each night when we were on our backpack trips.

I thought Tyson was gonna have a heart attack when he heard. "In bear country!" he choked on the water he was drinking as he said it. "Are you crazy? Do you know how dangerous that was?"

"Yeah... but you made it so good that..."

"Are you serious?"

"Yeah, but nothing happened, so… it's fine."

"Do you know how lucky you are?"

"Yeah."

"Do you realize how much danger you put your tent mates in?"

"Um, yeah but…"

"Yeah-but! Yeah-but? What the hell is a yeah-but anyways?"

Paul looked at Tyson without a clue to what he was talking about. I could tell Paul was picturing what a 'yeah-but' might look like, as if it were a distant cousin of the bunny rabbit or something. All any of us could do was laugh. That was Paul.

Tyson chuckled to himself, "I am going to miss you Paul. I'm really going to miss you."

"Oh, thanks." Paul gleefully replied as if it was the best compliment he ever received. Then after a long pause he added, "I mean, um, I'm gonna miss you too. I mean all of you… yeah."

And he was proud of himself for saying so.

Jeff chimed in, "I'll miss you most of all, Scarecrow," but the reference was lost on Paul so no one else laughed either to save Paul's feelings from getting hurt.

11 am: Before the second group left I went to one of the shops in the airport. I bought Sarah a keychain with a bear standing on top of the word Alaska. I knew it was cheesy, but it was all I could afford. I know this might sound bad but I've never really given anyone a gift before. Not on my own without a birthday or something for a

reason at least. It felt good, better than I thought it would. Seeing the smile she cracked when I gave it to her was what felt so nice.

The second group was called to board their plane and we all hugged one last time.

Jeff wouldn't stop thanking Andrea and Tyson for everything they had done. He went on and on about his old camp and how the leaders were tyrants who weren't afraid of issuing a little corporal punishment from time to time. Jeff talked about how their rationale to the campers was always the same, "When you become a counselor it will be your turn to do the same thing to your campers. That's how you can get even."

Jeff explained that this sort of behavior was, for the most part, accepted as status quo at his old camp, commonly perceived as a rite of passage, a running through the gauntlet. But in reality it was nothing more than the completion of a vicious circle, the passing down of traumatizing experiences from one generation to the next. The bullification of society. And that it could happen anywhere.

I knew that I had helped perpetuate the same kind of thing back home, and I felt terrible for that. But living in the past wouldn't help. Learning from it was the key. I vowed to myself that I would never again repeat the cycle of fear and hate. I would be one of the people leading the way to help break it.

I hugged Matt and promised to keep in touch. I thanked him for sticking up for me that day when we tried to summit the peak. He smiled and thanked me for standing up for Lucy. It felt good realizing I had made a friendship that would last the rest of my life. I figured I had made a few of those. Then I kissed Sarah goodbye and thanked her for everything. And then she was gone. So was everyone else.

1:15 pm: I am on a flight by myself and was the last one to leave. When it was time to go, I thanked Tyson and Andrea again for everything. They wished me luck. I told Tyson that I didn't know what was going to happen to me once I got home, but that I knew I would be able to handle it, life, whatever came my way.

Tyson smiled and offered up some parting wisdom he stole from his hero, "Remember what Bob Dylan said once, 'All I can do is be me, whoever that is.'"

I tried to imitate Tyson's chuckle, then walked down the gate to load the plane. I sat down and looked out the window to the distant mountains.

I will forever long for this wild and free place, Alaska. I will always remember the people who gave me the opportunity to discover that it is okay to be me.

ABOUT THE AUTHOR

Dan Zahn is a writer with a truly artistic soul: a sailor in search of the perfect vessel. Chasing life and experience around the globe, he is driven by philosophical ideas as well as whim and fancy. Always embracing knowledge and understanding, Dan is a student of life seeking to share illumination where the world is dark.